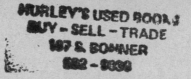
A Cool Mind Stood Between Ole Devil and Death . . .

The shorter of the braves drew his knife. Stepping into position, he dug the fingers of his other hand into Ole Devil's hair. With a savage jerk, he snatched the Texian into a sitting position. Searing pain which seemed to be setting the top of his skull on fire brought tears involuntarily to Ole Devil's eyes, but he managed to hold back the yelp of torment that the sensation almost caused. At any moment, he expected to feel the knife's blade biting into his flesh. It would not be a mortal thrust, but merely designed to hurt.

Sucking in a breath, Ole Devil prepared to resist any inclination to cry out. If possible, he meant to die well. However, before he did, he must give Villena some satisfactory yet untrue explanation for his presence. Not only would it have to be believable, but it would have to send the Mexican as far away as possible from Santa Cristóbal Bay and the route to be taken by the mule train.

Books by J. T. Edson

THE NIGHTHAWK
NO FINGER ON THE TRIGGER
THE BAD BUNCH
SLIP GUN
TROUBLED RANGE
THE FASTEST GUN IN TEXAS
THE HIDE AND TALLOW MEN
THE JUSTICE OF COMPANY Z
MCGRAW'S INHERITANCE
RAPIDO CLINT
COMANCHE
A MATTER OF HONOR
RENEGADE
WACO RIDES IN
BLOODY BORDER
ALVIN FOG, TEXAS RANGER
HELL IN THE PALO DURO
OLE DEVIL AT SAN JACINTO
GO BACK TO HELL
OLE DEVIL AND THE MULE TRAIN
VIRIDIAN'S TRAIL

Ole Devil and the Caplocks

J. T. EDSON

A DELL BOOK

Published by
Dell Publishing
a division of
Bantam Doubleday Dell Publishing Group, Inc.
666 Fifth Avenue
New York, New York 10103

ISBN: 0-440-21042-9

Printed in the United States of America

Published simultaneously in Canada

February 1993

10   9   8   7   6   5   4   3   2   1

OPM

To Chuck and Ellen Kurtzman of Fort Worth, Texas, with fond memories of many a filling of Ubert with "Limpopo Water."

Author's Note

While complete in themselves, events in this book continue from those recorded in *Young Ole Devil*. Although readers have been promised more information about the composition and operation of a Mule Train, regretfully space has not permitted me to include it in this book, but I promise it will be given in *Ole Devil and the Mule Train* (not, as stated in various footnotes, in *Ole Devil at San Jacinto*).

1
THEY COULD CHANGE HISTORY

Having been carried in by the sea breeze and flowing tide shortly before noon on February 26, 1836, the two-masted trading brig *Bostonian Lady* was rocking gently at its anchor. There was an air of urgency about the actions of the sailors who were starting to transfer some of the cargo from the forward hold to the boats which had been lowered. Although Captain Adams had not offered any explanation, they realized that only exceptional circumstances could have caused him to accept the navigational hazards of bringing his vessel into the small, landlocked, Santa Cristóbal Bay. Situated about ten miles north of the Matagordá Peninsula, it was in what was usually an unpopulated region. The nearest human habitation was the tiny port of San Phillipe, which they had passed on their southbound course some fifteen miles farther up the Texas coast.

From all appearances, the captain had not been surprised to find human beings at the bay. In fact, his behavior had suggested that he was expecting to find somebody in what should have been a deserted area. On approaching the coast-line, he had studied the mouth of the bay through his telescope. Although they did not have similar aids to vision, a couple of the hands claimed they had seen a man waving what appeared to be a blanket from the cliffs above the entrance. Despite this signal, Adams had not entered immediately. Instead, the *Bostonian Lady* had hove to offshore for almost an hour. During that period he had climbed the main mast and searched the horizon; presumably to satisfy himself that there were no other vessels within visual distance. When sure that they were unobserved, he had descended and given orders to go in.

On entering the bay, there had been indisputable evidence that the visit was prearranged. Several men were gathered on the beach and the brig's sole passenger had been sent ashore in the jolly boat. As soon as he had landed, orders had been given that had set the crew to work.

Few of the sailors took much interest in current affairs unless the issues involved were such as might affect them personally, but even the most disinterested of them could not help being aware that at that time there was some kind of serious trouble taking place in Texas. It had been the main topic of conversation around New Orleans for several months past. None of the fo'c's'le hands had extensive knowledge of why the Anglo-Saxon colonists and not a few *Chicanos** had elected to sever all connections with Mexico and establish a self-governing Republic under the Lone Star flag.† Nor did they particularly care. What did concern them was an uneasy feeling that the local authorities would not approve, to put it mildly, of their visit.

The suspicion had been strengthened when the sailors were told which items of the cargo to extract from the hold. The designated boxes had caused comment and speculation

---

* Chicano: *a Mexican, or Spanish-born citizen of Texas.*
† *The reason for the colonists' decision is explained at length in* YOUNG OLE DEVIL.

after they had been loaded at New Orleans. Some were oblong, about five foot in length, three wide, three deep, and heavy. The rest were lighter and roughly three foot square. All had one significant point in common. There was nothing on them to say what their contents might be, from whence they had come, nor to where and whom they were to be delivered.

However, the hands knew better than to mention their misgivings openly. Captain Nathaniel Adams was a humane, tolerant and easy-going man—in comparison with many of his class—but he would not—could not—permit the members of his crew to question his actions. So they set to work as quickly as possible in order to reduce the length of time they must spend in such a potentially precarious location.

Fortunately for the crew, none of them stopped to think too deeply about their situation. Having arrived at their destination at the commencement of the incoming tide and with the breeze blowing from the sea toward the land, the *Bostonian Lady* would have difficulty in leaving before the ebb. Even after the tide had turned, it might be necessary to tow the brig out to sea with her boats. Going out before the ebb would be a slow and laborious task. Too slow, in all probability, for them to escape if anything should go wrong.

Captain Adams had a better appreciation of the position. While he was not fully cognizant with the causes of the strife which was embroiling Texas, he knew that carrying out the mission which had brought him to Santa Cristóbal Bay was placing himself and his vessel in considerable jeopardy. If he should be caught, the very least he could expect was for the *Bostonian Lady* to be impounded. From what he knew of Latin officials—and he had seen plenty of them during his years of trading from the *Rio Bravo** in the north, via Cuba

* Rio Bravo: *the Mexicans' name for the Rio Grande.*

and Puerto Rico, as far as the *Rio de la Plata* in South America—his fate was likely to be far worse than that. He had been well paid, with the certainty of other and less risky cargoes in the future. Arrangements, which appeared to be working, had been made to reduce the risks but he knew that there was still danger and he would not be sorry when he could get under way. Once he was out at sea, it would be very difficult for the Mexican authorities to prove that he had been connected with the unmarked consignment.

"I've got the cargo broken out and am having it put into the boats, Cap'n," announced the mate, having come from the forward hold to where his superior was standing amidships studying the beach through a telescope. "So I hope yon fancy dressed supercargo* knows what he's talking about."

"He said he knew the party who were waiting, Mister Shrift," Adams pointed out. "And he wouldn't be fool enough to go ashore unless he was certain that everything's all right. You can start sending his consignment across."

"Aye aye, sir," the mate assented and returned to supervise the work.

For all the captain's comment, he felt perturbed. The men who had hired him had laid great emphasis upon the need for secrecy and that their consignment must not be permitted to fall into the wrong hands. In spite of having received the correct signal from the cliffs and his passenger's assurance that all was well, he was uneasy when he thought of the reception committee. While none of the quartet who had come to the water's edge looked like Mexicans, neither did they appear to be a delegation from the Republic of Texas; particularly when something so important was involved.

While the man at the left of the party most assuredly was

* Supercargo: an agent placed on board a ship to be in charge of the purchase, sale, or safe delivery of a consignment. Often used as a derogatory term by sailors.

not of Latin origin, neither did he spring from Anglo-Saxon stock. In fact, despite Adams's entire sea service having been confined to the eastern side of the American continent and its offshore islands, he was able to recognize that the man was a native of the Orient.

Not quite five foot six in height, but with a sturdy build, the Oriental was young. Bareheaded, his black hair was close cropped and he had sallow, almond-eyed, cheerful features. His garments were a loose fitting black shirt hanging outside trousers of a similar material which were tucked into matching Hessian boots.† Apart from his footwear and the lack of a pigtail, he might have been a Chinese coolie such as could be seen in most of the United States's major seaports. However, one rarely saw a coolie carrying weapons and he appeared to be well, if primitively, armed. A pair of long hilted, slightly curved swords with small circular guards hung—the shorter at the right—with their sheaths attached by slings to his leather waistbelt. In addition, he held a long bow in his left hand and a quiver hanging across his right shoulder pointed the flights of several arrows so they would be readily accessible when required.

Adams found the second member of the quartet equally puzzling, but in a different way. About three or four inches taller than the Oriental, the snug fit of a fringed buckskin shirt, trousers and rawhide moccasins left no doubt that—in spite of a pistol thrust through the right side of a belt which also had a knife hanging at the left in an Indian-made sheath —it was a girl in her late teens and fast approaching the full bloom of womanhood. Her fiery red and curly hair had been cut fairly short. For all that the right eye was blackened and the top lip swollen, her pretty, freckled face expressed a

† *Hessian boots: designed for riding, with legs extending to just below the knee and having a V-shaped notch at the front; originally used by light cavalry such as Hussars.*

happy-go-lucky zest for life. While the attire was unconventional to say the least for a member of her sex, it seemed to suit her personality, and, somehow, the weapons she was carrying did not appear incongruous in her possession.

From the similarity of their clothing, the remaining pair were apparently clad in some type of uniform. Hanging on their shoulders by *barbiquejo* chinstraps, they had black hats of the low crowned, wide brimmed pattern which had become popular as *Presidente* Antonio Lopez de Santa Anna's repressive and obstructive policies had caused a growing antipathy among young Texians* toward everything of Mexican origin. Their buckskin shirts were tucked into tight legged fawn riding breeches and they had on Hessian boots. A pistol carried in a broad, slanting leather loop on the right side of the belt had its butt turned forward so as to be available to either hand. It was balanced by a massive knife of the kind which had already acquired the name "bowie"† in honor of the man who was credited with designing the original weapon. There was only one noticeable difference in the pair's attire. The man next to the girl sported a long, tightly rolled bandana that was a riot of clashing colors while his companion's was plain scarlet.

At least six foot tall, the man with the scarlet bandana appeared to be in his early twenties. Bulky of build, he conveyed an impression of well padded, contented lethargy. He had curly auburn hair and there was an amiable expression on his sun-reddened face.

Unless Adams missed his guess, the remaining member of the group was its leader. Matching his Anglo-Saxon compan-

---

* Texian: an Anglo-U.S.-born citizen of Texas, the "i" being dropped from general usage after annexation by the United States and the Mexican War of 1846–48.
† What happened to James Bowie's knife after his death at the conclusion of the siege of the Alamo Mission—at San Antonio de Bexar, Texas, on March 6, 1836—is told in THE QUEST FOR BOWIE'S BLADE.

ion's size and about the same age, he had a whipcord lean physique. He stood with a straight-backed alertness that was emphasized by the other's almost slouching posture. However, it was his features which the captain found most interesting. Combed back above the temples, his black hair seemed to form two small, curved horns. Taken with eyebrows like inverted "V's," a neatly trimmed mustache and a short, sharp pointed chin beard, either accidentally or deliberately the protuberances made his lean, tanned, otherwise handsome face look like the accepted conception of the Devil's physiognomy.

Even from a distance of close to a quarter of a mile, aided by the magnification of his powerful telescope, Adams's shrewd judgment of human nature led him to determine that the slender young man bore the undefinable and yet recognizable aura of a born leader. He comported himself with assurance, but there was no trace of self-conscious arrogance which frequently marked a less competent person who had been placed in a position of authority. In spite of that, he struck the captain as being an unusual choice for so important a task as collecting and delivering the consignment.

Despite appreciating how vital the goods in his charge might prove to be in the Texians' struggle for independence, the "supercargo" had not shared Adams's qualms. In fact, Beauregard Rassendyll had been delighted when—using a borrowed telescope as the brig was approaching its anchorage—he had discovered who was to be his escort. He had not hesitated to request that he be taken ashore, or in confirming that the consignment could be landed. What was more, his only slight misgivings were relieved by the conversation which took place shortly after he had stepped from the jolly boat.

"Beau!" greeted the slender young man, striding forward with his right hand held out. "I thought it was you, but

Cousin Mannen said Uncle Marsden couldn't be so short of reliable help that he'd need to send *you.*"

"Huh!" Rassendyll sniffed, looking all around the bay with an overexaggerated care. "I was told I'd have a suitable escort waiting. You wouldn't have seen them, would you, Devil?"

In spite of the comments, there was pleasure on the two young men's faces as their hands met and shook. Then they studied each other as friends would when meeting after a lengthy separation.

Studying the most obvious change in Jackson Baines Hardin's appearance, Rassendyll felt puzzled. There had always been a slightly Mephistophelian aspect to his features, which in part had produced his nickname "Ole Devil,"* but the hornlike effect caused by the way his hair was combed, the mustache and beard, tended to emphasize it. Being aware of the circumstances which had compelled him to come to Texas, the supercargo would have expected him to avoid anything that made him easily identifiable.

Returning the scrutiny, Ole Devil found little change in Rassendyll. His senior by four years, the supercargo topped him by about three inches and, although not as bulky as Mannen Blaze, was more heavily built. Red haired, clean shaven and handsome, clad in a white "planter's" hat and riding clothes cut in the latest fashion popular among the wealthy young Southrons of Louisiana, he looked as hard and fit as when they had served together on a merchant ship commanded by Ole Devil's father.

"They've sent you *the* best," the Mephistophelian-featured Texian declared, releasing his right hand so that he could indicate a group of about twenty well-armed men in similar attire to his own. They were standing about two hundred

*A more important cause of Jackson Baines Hardin's nickname was his well-deserved reputation for being a "lil ole devil" in a fight.

yards away, with a number of excellent quality horses. "Isn't that right, Cousin Mannen?"

"You've never been righter, Cousin Devil," confirmed Mannen Blaze, in a sleepy drawl that matched his lethargic attitude, having ambled forward to his kinsman's side. However, there was nothing weak or tired in his grip as he shook the supercargo's hand. "You ask most anybody, Beau, and see what they say about Company 'C' of the Texas Light Cavalry."

"I'd hate to, if there were ladies present," Rassendyll stated, glancing past the Texians in a pointed manner. "Hello there, Tommy—ma'am."

"This is an old friend of ours, Beauregard Rassendyll, from New Orleans, Di," Ole Devil introduced, taking the hint and presenting the supercargo to the girl and the little Oriental. "I wish I could say he was kin, you can't pick them. Beau, I'd like you to meet Diamond-Hitch Brindley. She and her grandfather are handling the transportation of the consignment."

A keen student of women, Rassendyll had been examining the girl with interest. While she was not yet twenty and dressed in a most unusual manner, there was little of the shy, naive, backwoods maiden about her. Nor, despite the revealing nature of her garments, did she appear brazen and wanton. Instead, her whole attitude was redolent of self-confident competence. It implied that she was used to the company of men and dealing with them as equals, neither ignoring nor playing upon the fact that she was an attractive member of the opposite sex.

The supercargo was aware that he was being studied and analyzed just as thoroughly, and he found the sensation a trifle disconcerting. Normally he would have enjoyed being stared at by such a good-looking and shapely person, but on this occasion he deduced that it was not for the usual flattering reasons. She was not contemplating him with a view to a possible romance. Rather she was considering him as a man would consider another member of his sex who would be accompanying him upon a hazardous endeavor. He was as yet an unknown quantity who might prove more of a liability than an asset. From her attitude it appeared that while she was willing to accept him as the friend of somebody for whom she had considerable respect, he would have to win her approbation on his own merits.

"I'm not *so* old, Miss Brindley," Rassendyll corrected, offering his hand. He wondered how the girl had come by such a strange Christian name and how she had received the injuries to her face. "It's just that knowing this pair has aged me."

"Likely," Charlotte Jane Martha Brindley admitted, shaking hands. "Only the name's 'Di,' which's short for 'Diamond-Hitch' and I'm called that because I can throw one faster, tighter 'n' better than anybody, man, woman, or child. How soon'll we be getting 'em over here, Beau?"

"The crew should be fetching the first of them in the next few minutes," Rassendyll replied, having been impressed by the strength and hardness of her hand. "Are your wagons coming down?"

"We're using mules, not wagons," Ole Devil put in. "It was decided that they'd be quicker and better suited to our needs."

"Grandpappy Ewart's fetching 'em along," Di went on. "But we figured's how we'd best come ahead to make sure it'd be safe for them to be landed."

"And I presume that it is safe," Rassendyll remarked, making the words a statement rather than a question.

"It is," Di confirmed. "Now."

"Did you run into trouble, Devil?" Rassendyll inquired, swinging around to look at the Texian.

"Some," Ole Devil admitted, but nothing could be read from his Mesphistophelian features to suggest just how serious the trouble might have been. "With any luck, it's all over now."

"Huh!" snorted Di. "The way those damned renegades lit out, they won't dare come back and, after what Tommy did to it, that blasted Mexican ship'll not be able to."

"Renegades," the supercargo repeated. *"Ship!"*

"There were a bunch of renegades around," Ole Devil explained. "But Cousin Mannen arrived with Company 'C' and drove them off. We found a ten-gun brig taking on water in the bay, but we tricked its captain into leaving. It went south and, provided we don't have any delays, we should have finished here and the ship'll be gone before it could beat back."

"If I know Captain Adams, there won't be any delays. He knows too well what will happen to him if he's caught," Rassendyll stated, then glanced at the men with the horses. Knowing something of the Republic of Texas's newly formed army, he continued, "Is that your full company?"

"Less than half of it," Ole Devil answered in a reassuring manner. "I've sent twenty-five men to the mule train in case they should be needed. The rest are beyond the rim, some keeping watch from the cliffs in case that Mexican brig comes back, the rest acting as pickets on the range."

"Good," Rassendyll praised, finding that his misgivings about the small size of the escort were groundless. "If you'll bring the mules down, we can start loading them as soon as the consignment arrives from the brig."

"It's not that easy," Di warned. "You can't move pack mules as quickly as riding hosses. So Grandpappy Ewart won't be able to get 'em here afore sundown at the soonest."

"Sundown?" Rassendyll repeated, glancing at the sky as if

J. T. EDSON

to estimate how much longer they would have to wait. "Adams won't agree to stay in the bay until then."

"He doesn't need to," Ole Devil replied. "In fact, he can leave as soon as he's sent the consignment ashore. One of the reasons we came on ahead of the mule train was so he could land it and set sail again with the minimum of delay."

"On top of that," Di went on, bristling a little at what she regarded as the supercargo's implied criticism of their arrangements, "we figure on having the rifles packed ready for moving when Grandpappy Ewart gets here."

"There's no need for *that*," Rassendyll protested. "We aren't carrying them loose, they're in boxes of twenty-four."

"Our mules can tote twenty-four apiece all right, but not while they're in a wooden box," Di countered, and the supercargo could sense that the conversation was doing nothing to improve her opinion of him. "So we aim to take 'em out and put 'em in bundles of twelve."

"Can you get us enough canvas from the ship to wrap them in, Beau?" Ole Devil inquired, hiding the amusement he was feeling over having noticed the girl's attitude toward his friend and recollecting that she had treated him in a similar fashion on their first meeting. "We were traveling fast and couldn't bring anything with us to make up the bundles."

"I'll ask the captain to send some over," Rassendyll promised. "I was told that I could make any purchases which might be necessary."

"*Bueno,*" Ole Devil drawled.

"You called it right, Beau," Mannen put in, before his cousin could continue. "They're surely not wasting any time. Here comes the first load."

Propelled by four sailors, a boat was making a swift passage between the *Bostonian Lady* and the shore. At Ole Devil's signal, the men of his company left their horses standing ground-hitched by allowing the split-ended reins to dangle and walked to the beach. Without needing orders, they waded to where the boat had been brought to a halt. Taking hold of an oblong box's rope handles, two of them lifted and carried it on to dry land.

"Open them up, Sergeant Grayne," Ole Devil instructed to a stocky, bearded man who had no insignia of rank but was standing aside with a short crowbar in his hand.

"Yo!" the non-com replied, giving what was already the accepted cavalryman's response to an order.

Prying open the box's lid, Grayne exposed its contents to view. Twenty-four rifles lay inside, their butts in alternating directions. Lifting one out, the girl examined it without worrying about the grease with which it was coated. About four foot in length, with a barrel thirty-six inches long and .53 in caliber, it looked a typical "plains" rifle developed with the needs of travelers west of the Mississippi River in mind. However, she noticed that there were three main differences between it and the weapons to which she was accustomed. Most obvious, at the breech, the hammer had a flattened head with no jaws for holding a flint and, instead of a frizzen pan, there was only a small protuberance with a nipple on top as a means of igniting the powder charge in the chamber. The third difference was a metal stud on the side of the barrel slightly over an inch from the muzzle.

"It's a fair piece," Di stated with the air of a connoisseur after several seconds, and she indicated the stud. "But I've never seen a doohickey like this afore."

"It's to fix a bayonet on, there's one for each of them in the bottom of the boxes," Rassendyll explained. "A company in the United States made them, hoping to sell them to the army, but the generals didn't want anything as newfangled as caplocks."

"Which is lucky for Texas," Ole Devil declared. "Provided

we can get them to General Houston, they could change history."

"Then we'd best be getting to doing something more than standing and talking," Di announced, replacing the rifle and wiping her hands on her thighs.

"I'll go and make arrangements for the canvas," Rassendyll offered.

"*Bueno,*" the girl replied. "We can start splitting 'em into twelves, Devil."

Crossing to the *Bostonian Lady* in the jolly boat, Rassendyll bought sufficient canvas for Di's purpose. On his return to the shore, he found the work of making the consignment ready for onwards transportation was being carried out. So he took the opportunity to pass on some private information which he was sure Ole Devil would be very pleased to receive.

"Kerry Vanderlyne has proved who killed Saul Beaucoup, Devil," the supercargo said, having taken his friend beyond the hearing of the rest of the party. "That clears your name. There's nothing to stop you going back to Louisiana."

2

THERE COULD BE *NO* GOING BACK!

"That clears your name. There's nothing to stop you going back to Louisiana."

Beauregard Rassendyll's words still seemed to be keeping time with the big linebacked dun gelding's two-beat gait—wherein the off fore and near hind and the near fore and off hind alternately struck the ground at the same time—and Ole Devil Hardin tried to shake them from his thoughts as he rode "posting the trot"* into an area of woodland some five miles southwest of Santa Cristóbal Bay. They had been so perturbing that, wanting to consider them without distraction, he had left Diamond-Hitch Brindley, Mannen Blaze and the supercargo to attend to the consignment of caplock rifles while he, ostensibly, made the rounds of the pickets.

While Rassendyll's news had been very welcome in one respect, from another it had presented its recipient with the making of a very difficult decision.

* *A detailed description of how to ride "posting the trot" is given in the "The Scout" episode of* UNDER THE STARS AND BARS.

From the beginning of the affair that had caused Ole Devil to come to Texas, but he could have proved that he was innocent of Saul Beaucoup's murder but for one vitally important detail. He had had a perfect alibi, except that he could only use it by besmirching the honor of the woman he loved and creating a situation which could have had grave repercussions throughout the whole State of Louisiana.

Not that Melissa Cornforth would have objected, or refused to help Ole Devil. In fact, she had begged him to ignore the consequences and allow her to do so. Despite the precarious nature of his position, he had declined to accept her suggestion. He had appreciated the ramifications of permitting her to compromise herself. They went far beyond the disastrous effect which such an action would have had upon her social standing and future.

As was frequently done by upper-class Southrons, Melissa's parents had arranged what they considered to be a suitable and mutually advantageous marriage for her. Apart from one factor, she would have been content to conform with their wishes. The man in question was Kerry Vanderlyne, whom she had known since they were children. He was handsome and, while there had been no romantic feeling between them, she had always been on the best of terms with him. Unfortunately, shortly before their betrothal was announced, she had met and fallen in love with his best friend —Jackson Baines Hardin.

Hoping to find some way of resolving the situation without hurting or embarrassing Vanderlyne, of whom they were both fond, Melissa and Ole Devil had met secretly to discuss it in an unoccupied cabin on the boundary separating her parents' and his uncle's plantations. Caught by an unexpected and violent thunderstorm, they were compelled to spend the night there. Although Melissa had contrived to return home the following morning without anybody discovering what had happened, a serious complication had arisen.

During the night, a wealthy Iberville Parish* bully and trouble-causer, Saul Beaucoup, had been murdered in Crown Bayou.

In spite of his family's social prominence, Kerry Vander-lyne, having become interested in law enforcement, was serving as town constable and deputy sheriff in Crown Bayou. So it had fallen upon him to conduct the investigation. All the available evidence had suggested that Ole Devil was the culprit. There was known to be ill will between him and Beaucoup and a sword belonging to him was buried in the other's back. What was more, while unable to make a positive identification, a witness claimed to have seen a man answering to Ole Devil's general description hurrying away from the scene of the crime at about eleven o'clock the previous evening.

When questioned by Vanderlyne, Ole Devil had stated he was innocent. The sword was one of half a dozen he had brought with him and had been in the *salle de armes* at the Blaze plantation from where it could easily have been removed without the loss being noticed. However, he had refused to account for his movements at the time that the murder was being committed.

There had been excellent reasons for Ole Devil's reticence and refusal to let Melissa speak on his behalf. When her parents heard what had happened, they would never forgive him even if he married her. Nor, no matter how Vanderlyne accepted the loss of his fiancée, would the rest of his kin. As the two families formed a powerful support for the Hardin, Fog and Blaze clan in the state's affairs, he had no desire to

* The State of Louisiana uses the term "parish" instead of "county."

bring such an advantageous alliance to an end if it could be avoided.

Although convinced of Ole Devil's innocence, Vanderlyne had been forced to take him into custody. Failure to have done so would have been contrary to the oath the young man had sworn on becoming a peace officer. In addition, it would have antagonized the Beaucoup family and their friends who were hinting that justice would not be done. So a refusal would have embroiled the citizens of Crown Bayou and the parish seat, Plaguemine, in the controversy. With so many influential people involved, most of Louisiana's population would probably have taken sides. Once that had happened, a feud of statewide proportions and costing many lives was almost certain to have developed.

Being an intelligent girl, Melissa had not blamed Vanderlyne for arresting Ole Devil. She had also understood the latter's reason for insisting that she did not become involved, even to prove his innocence. Yet, with so much of the evidence suggesting that he was guilty, she was determined to save him. Taking Mannen Blaze into her confidence, she had found that he was willing to help her. However, neither of them had been able to decide what to do. The arrival of one of Melissa's cousins had provided them with a solution. Telling Rezin Pleasant Bowie* the full story, she had obtained his support. A shrewd man, he had produced a plan. Aided by Mannen, he had broken Ole Devil out of jail. No suspicion of his part had fallen upon Bowie. The cousins had fled to Texas, joining others of their kin who had already settled there and were taking an active interest in that area of Mexico's affairs.†

* *Rezin Pleasant Bowie, elder brother of James, q.v., and believed by many authorities to have been the actual designer of the "bowie" knife.*
† *During the period in question, Texas was regarded by the Mexican Government as being a Territory of the State of Coahuila. Santa Anna's refusal*

While the Beaucoup faction had been furious when they heard of the escape and had offered a large reward for the capture of Ole Devil and Mannen, nothing worse had happened. Tactfully, as the bounty said "Alive Only," the Hardin, Fog and Blaze clan had not protested at its issue. So, having no desire to antagonize such a powerful confederation, the Beaucoups had announced publicly that they accepted that the jail-delivery had been engineered by the two young men without the knowledge, authority or assistance of their family. With an apology from Ole Devil's and Mannen's fathers, made without any admission that the former might have been guilty, the affair had been allowed to come to a peaceful end.**

As Vanderlyne had been handling a matter of law enforcement on the Beaucoups' behalf some distance from Crown Bayou at the time of the escape, one of the factors which Bowie had taken into consideration, his career as a peace officer, had not suffered on account of it. Not only was he retained in office—much to the annoyance of his father, who did not approve of him carrying out such work—but two years later he had been elected sheriff of Iberville Parish. He had continued to search for the truth about the killing, believing that—in spite of Ole Devil's escape and flight—some other person was responsible.

The discovery that he had finally been proven innocent was a great relief to Ole Devil. Not only had his conscience been troubled by his having escaped from jail, although he had had more than his own welfare in mind when agreeing,

---

to make it a State in its own right, with full representation in the national government, was one of the reasons for the Texians' resentment and bitterness.
** In the author's opinion, the fact that the Beaucoup family did not take the matter any further suggests they suspected—or knew—the wrong man was being blamed.

but he had hated the stigma which he felt his actions had put upon his name. On learning of the price which had been put on his head by the Beaucoups, he had adopted the hornlike style for his hair and cultivated the mustache and beard. He had always been aware of his features' somewhat Mephistophelian characteristics. So he had sought to emphasize them in spite of warnings from others of his family that they would draw attention and remind people of his nickname. It had not been a mere act of braggadocio, but was a subconscious wish to prove that—although he might have "gone to Texas"*—he had no reason to conceal his true identity.

However, the rest of Rassendyll's news had caused the young Texian considerable mental turmoil and heart-searching.

Being aware of the consequences if he should return to Louisiana with the murder charge still hanging over him and having had no hope that his name would be cleared by the discovery of the real culprit's identity, Ole Devil had reconciled himself to making his home in Texas. Nor was there any chance of Melissa joining him. They had decided that at their last meeting, on the road west out of Crown Bayou just after he had made his escape from the town's jail. For her to have followed him would have meant the end of her engagement with Vanderlyne and the creation of the dissension between their respective families which they were trying to prevent. So they had put their duty to their kinfolk before their love for each other and had parted. Nor had they made any attempt to communicate and he had heard little about her until Rassendyll's arrival.

While far from being promiscuous, having accepted that Melissa was in all probability lost to him, Ole Devil had not

* "Gone to Texas": at odds with the law in the United States. Many wanted men entered Texas in the period before annexation, knowing that there was little danger of them being caught and extradited by the Mexican authorities.

entirely shunned contact with members of the opposite sex since settling in Texas. Nor had the opportunity to meet them been lacking. Despite knowing why he had been compelled to leave Louisiana, or at least such of the facts as had been made public, he was still considered an eligible bachelor by virtue of his influential connections. More than one family had sought to interest him in its unmarried daughters, cousins or nieces. However, not one of the young ladies with whom he had become acquainted had drawn even close to replacing Melissa in his affections. What was more, according to the supercargo's story, there was a chance that she reciprocated his feelings.

Although Melissa and Vanderlyne were still engaged, it had been announced that they did not intend to marry until he was in a position to support her in something close to the manner to which she was accustomed. The reason for the delay was that he had become estranged from his father by his insistence on remaining a peace officer and refusing to accept financial assistance from her parents. He had been so successful during his period in the capacity of sheriff of Iberville Parish that he was to be appointed U.S. Marshal for the State of Louisiana. Such an important post had brought a reconciliation with his father and would also allow him to take Melissa for his bride.

The date set for Vanderlyne's appointment was the thirty-first of March!

Everybody who knew the couple was expecting that their wedding would follow shortly, probably before the end of April!

With his innocence established, Ole Devil was free to return to Louisiana and renew his relationship with the only woman he had ever loved. However, apart from any other consideration, he would have to leave Texas as soon as possi-

ble if he wanted to arrive before she was lost to him forever
by becoming Vanderlyne's wife.

Unfortunately, Ole Devil had appreciated that there were
a number of obstacles in the path of his desire. One of the
most important was the realization that he now owed an additional debt to Vanderlyne. Thinking about his and Mannen's flight, he had always suspected the peace officer had
failed to act with his usual diligence and efficiency when or-
ganizing the pursuit after the jail-delivery. Now it was clear
that he had continued to devote time and effort to clearing
his friend's name.

Such an obligation was not to be taken lightly by a man of
Ole Devil's character, background and upbringing.

What was more, there were others to whom the young
Texian was under a debt of gratitude.

The Bowie family had a claim upon Ole Devil for the part
one of them had played in his escape. Not only had Rezin
Pleasant Bowie planned how it was to be done, he had risked
his liberty and reputation by helping Mannen Blaze to imple-
ment the far from danger-free scheme.

Being members of the Hardin, Fog and Blaze clan had
done much to smooth the two young fugitives' path across
Louisiana, as had the money and other aids to the flight
which had been supplied without question when Mannen had
requested them. Other kinsmen, accepting Ole Devil's word
that he was innocent, had helped the cousins to establish
themselves in Texas. He knew and shared their sentiments on
the matter of breaking free from the tyrannical yoke of *Presidente* Antonio Lopez de Santa Anna and had committed
himself, without pressure from them to do so, to the cause.

Bearing the latter point in mind, Ole Devil had his well-
developed sense of duty to contend with. He was all too
aware of how badly the hurriedly formed, greatly outnum-

bered Army of the Republic of Texas needed every man. Harassed by internal friction as much as from the enemy, Major General Samuel Houston could ill afford to lose the services of a loyal, disciplined and competent officer, which Ole Devil knew he had proved himself to be.

In addition, there was Melissa's feelings for Ole Devil to consider. While the delay in the marriage might have been at her instigation and caused by the hope that circumstances might allow him to return and resume their love affair, it could also be for the reason given by Rassendyll. It was in keeping with Vanderlyne's character that he would want to support his wife and by his own efforts rather than relying upon the bounty of his, or her, parents, and yet refuse to allow her standards of living to be lowered to any great extent.

So, in spite of his assumption that he could go back and take up where he had left off with Melissa, Ole Devil was realistic enough to concede that he might be wrong. In the years which had elapsed since his departure, she could have changed her attitude toward him. It was possible that she had come to love Vanderlyne and put Ole Devil from her thoughts as being unattainable. If he returned, he might stir up an emotional conflict which would be better avoided.

What was more, a successful resumption of their love affair would produce the friction between their respective families which Ole Devil's refusal to allow Melissa to prove his innocence in the first place had been intended to avert. The need to prevent it was even greater now than it had been when the incident occurred. The Cornforths and Vanderlynes were backing the Hardins, Fogs and Blazes in the bitter controversy over whether the United States Congress should continue to allow support to be given to the Texians in their struggle for independence.

The continuation of the powerful alliance between the families would be of far greater importance in the future. Many prominent Texians, Ole Devil's kin among them, accepted that the forming of an independent Republic was only a short-term policy. However, their ambition to see Texas become a part of the United States did not meet with complete approval in that country. The anti-slavery lobby was utterly, almost rabidly, opposed to what threatened to be the creation of further "Slave-States."* Others could not see any profit in the acquisition of such a vast, thinly populated, and, as far as they could tell, unproductive wilderness; particularly when obtaining it would antagonize and probably have an adverse effect upon trade with Mexico.

Taking all the facts into consideration, Ole Devil realized that his decision could have far-reaching effects. If Melissa was being forced against her wishes into an unwanted marriage with a man she hated, he would not have hesitated to return and take her regardless of the consequences. However, he knew that such was not the case. She had always felt warmth and affection, if not love, for Vanderlyne. In fact, her only misgivings over her feelings toward Ole Devil had been caused by a wish to avoid hurting her fiancé.

Being an intelligent young man, with a well-developed sense of responsibility, Ole Devil had known at the bottom of his heart from the moment he had heard Rassendyll's news that there was only one course he could take with honor. He must continue to adhere to the arrangement which Melissa and he had made that night on the outskirts of Crown Bayou.

There could be *no* going back!

Knowing it had been one thing, accepting it was less easy!

Although Ole Devil was normally too well adjusted to be

* The Texians had suggested that, considering the enormous area of land which would be involved, after annexation Texas could be divided into three or four separate states.

plagued by self-doubts, the receipt of the news and the understanding of its implications had been a traumatic experience. So much so that he had felt an irresistible desire to be alone and give the matter his undivided attention. Certainly the noise and activity on the beach at Santa Cristóbal Bay had been too distracting and disturbing for him to concentrate upon the various conflicting issues which were involved. Knowing that he could count upon Mannen, Di Brindley and Rassendyll as on himself, he had collected the gelding and, ostensibly, set off to inspect the pickets whom he had positioned earlier that morning.

None of the men Ole Devil had visited so far had had anything to report. However, in spite of approaching the most distant of the remaining pickets and knowing that it was the direction from which an enemy force might be expected to come, his emotional condition was making him far less alert and watchful than would normally have been the case.

An excellent horseman, the young Texian guided his horse through the woodland with hardly any need for conscious thought. He was following a trail which had been made either by wild animals or free-ranging longhorn cattle. Being well trained, the gelding kept far enough away from the trees to save him from banging his legs against the trunks or being swept from the saddle by low hanging branches.

Approaching a massive old cottonwood tree, the dun saw nothing to prevent it passing underneath the lowest branches. They were high enough for there to be no danger of them touching its rider. Still engrossed in his thoughts, Ole Devil was giving little attention to his surroundings. So the man who, having been concealed by the thick foliage, dropped off of an overhanging limb took him completely unawares.

Before the Texian could react, he was being half knocked and half dragged from his low horned, double girthed "slick fork" saddle.* Trying to struggle, his head struck the tree's trunk a glancing blow. For a brief instant, it seemed that bright lights were exploding inside his head. Then everything went black.

* *"Slick fork" saddle: one with little bulge, or roll, at the fork. Because of its Spanish connotations, the Texians preferred to use the word "girth" instead of "cinch."*

3
THEY'LL MAKE YOU TALK

"He's beginning to show signs of life at last. By the Holy Mother, that's fortunate for you. If you'd killed him, I would have made you wish you'd never been born."

The words, spoken in Spanish with the accent of an upper-class Mexican, seemed to be coming from a long way off. Yet for all his dazed and bewildered condition, Ole Devil Hardin could detect their hard and imperious timbre. Whoever was speaking appeared to be addressing his social inferiors.

"I'm pleased to see that you're recovering, *señor*," the voice continued, changing to English and picking the words carefully, as if the language was familiar but had not been used recently. "I was concerned when I first saw you, thinking you were more seriously injured by my man's attack."

Hearing his native tongue helped Ole Devil to clear his head of the mists which seemed to be swirling around in it, but nothing could dispel the nagging ache that was emanating from the back of his skull. However, with his faculties returning, he was able to appreciate that there was an underlying hardness to the polite and almost solicitous tones.

"Your hat cushioned at least some of the force with which

your head struck the trunk of the tree," the speaker went on, "otherwise the result would have been far worse. As it is, you have been unconscious for some minutes."

Gradually, the Texian's vision began to clear. From the sight which met his eyes and what he could feel, he was lying supine and far from comfortably on the ground. Above him spread the branches of the massive old cottonwood tree in which his unknown and, as yet, unseen assailant must have been concealed before dropping upon him.

Wanting to feel at his throbbing head in the hope that doing so would reduce the pain, Ole Devil tried to bring his hands from beneath his body. He found that he could not move them. For a few seconds, such was his befuddled state that he was unable to think why they were failing to respond to his will.

Then understanding struck him!

His wrists were bound together behind his back!

On experimenting, Ole Devil discovered that his ankles were also secured.

The Texian was not too surprised by the discovery. Already his brain was functioning sufficiently for him to deduce that, no matter how amiable the speaker might sound on the surface, he was unlikely to be an ally.

Shaking his head and gritting his teeth, Ole Devil raised his shoulders until he could examine his surroundings. As soon as his gaze was focused upon the speaker, he knew that the conclusions he had formed were correct. Standing with his legs apart, just clear of the Texian's feet, the man's attire was military in cut. It was not the uniform of any Mexican regiment with which Ole Devil was acquainted. Nor, despite there being a number of high-born *Chicanos* fighting against Santa Anna, did he believe the other was a member of the Republic of Texas's Army.

Slightly over medium height, the man's physique—empha-

sized by the cut of his expensive and well-tailored garments
—was reasonable if not exceptional. In his late twenties, his
deeply bronzed and handsome face had hazel eyes with
somewhat drooping lids and a Hapsburg* lip such as frequently occurred among members of high-class Spanish families. A Hussar-style black astrakhan† busby, with a silver
gray bag hanging out of its top behind a long, flowing plume
made of several emerald-green tail feathers from a cock
Quetzal,** had a golden cord passing around his neck from
the back. His form-fitting, waist long light green tunic was
elaborately frogged with black silk and the matching, tight-
legged breeches sported broad stripes of gold braid. The latter ended in black Wellington-legboots‡ with dangling gold
tassels at the front and large-roweled *"chihuahua"* spurs on
the low heels. A silver-gray coat, trimmed with black astrakhan, its sleeves empty, was draped across his shoulders.
However, instead of a cavalry saber, there was a magnificent
Toledo steel *épée-de-combat* attached to its slings on the left
side of his black leather waistbelt. As his hands—encased in
white gauntlets—were occupied, a heavy riding quirt dangled
by its strap from his left wrist.

   In spite of the way that the elegant—if somewhat travel-
stained—young man had spoken, Ole Devil sensed there was
something menacing about him. His dress and appearance

---

* *Hapsburg: an ancient German family from which were descended rulers
of Austria, Hungary and Bohemia, the Holy Roman Empire and Spain.*
† *Astrakhan: originally the pelts of very young lambs, with tightly curled
wool, from the district around the Russian city of that name. Later a fabric
with a curled pile in imitation of such pelts.*
** *Quetzal:* Pharomachrus Mocino, *one of the* Trogoniformes *birds, found
in the mountain forests of Central and South America regarded as sacred by
the Ancient Aztecs and Incas. Two of the cock's fringed tail covert feathers
may reach a length of over three feet, making them much sought after for
decorative purposes.*
‡ *Wellington-legboots: not the modern waterproofed rubber variety, but the
knee-length leather pattern made popular by the Duke of Wellington.*

marked him as being from a wealthy family of pure Spanish
blood. Since arriving in Texas, Ole Devil had met many of his
class. Some he had found to be gentlemen, even when judged
under the exacting standards by which he had been raised.
Others were race-proud, arrogant and vicious bullies. He
guessed that his captor was of the latter kind. Behind the
veneer of culture was a cold-blooded sadistic nature which
would take pleasure in inflicting pain.

Looking past the Mexican, Ole Devil discovered that they
were on the edge of a fair-sized clearing fringed with bushes
and trees.

And they were not alone!

Some twenty feet away, squatting on their heels in a rough
half circle and gazing at the Texian with coldly impassive
dark brown faces, were five tall, lean, and muscular Indians.
They had shoulder long black hair held back by cloth head-
bands which had no decoration such as feathers. Loose fitting, multicolored trade shirts hung outside deerskin breech-
cloths and the legs of their moccasins extended almost to
knee level.

Only one of the quintet possessed a firearm, the others
having either a knife in a sheath or a tomahawk's handle
thrust through the leather belts which encircled their shirts.
A couple nursed short bows and had quivers of arrows on
their backs. Three had flattish, slightly curved, sturdy pieces
of wood about twenty-four inches in length, which Ole Devil
identified as throwing sticks—simple, yet effective and
deadly weapons in skilled hands—by their sides. From all
appearances, the remaining member of the group was its
leader. Eldest and best dressed, with a red headband, he not
only had a knife, but there was a flintlock pistol tucked into
his belt and a nine-foot-long war lance standing with its head
spiked into the ground within easy reach of his right hand.

Although Ole Devil could not claim to be an authority on

such matters, he had always been a good listener, and he remembered what he was told. From the information given by men with more extensive knowledge, he decided that the Indians were Hopis. Hailing from the region of northwest Sonora known as "Arizona," they were one of the few tribes to employ throwing sticks as weapons.

There were a number of horses in the center of the clearing beyond the men, including the Texian's linebacked dun gelding which was ground hitched by its dangling, split-ended reins. The magnificent *palomino* gelding, with a floral patterned single girth saddle that had a swollen fork and a horn almost the size of a dinner plate, obviously belonged to the Mexican. It was standing a few feet away from the other animals, its one-piece reins held by an unarmed, barefooted Indian boy—who was shorter and more stocky than the Hopis, if that was their identity—clad in a battered straw *sombrero,* torn white cotton shirt and trousers with ragged legs.

With one exception, the rest of the animals were wiry Indian ponies of various colors. The latter had saddles with simple wooden trees covered by rawhide and war bridles made from a single length of rope fastened to the lower jaw by two half hitches. They were positioned so that Ole Devil could not see enough of the exception to make out how it was rigged. Nor did he waste time trying to find out.

Having given the Indians and the horses a quick examination, Ole Devil returned his attention to their Mexican companion and, almost certainly, superior. What he saw was not calculated to increase his peace of mind. Just the opposite, in fact.

The man was holding what at first glance appeared to be a so-called "Kentucky"* rifle, except that it had some unusual

* *The majority of the "Kentucky" rifles were actually made in Pennsylvania.*

features. One of the differences was that the hammer was underneath the frame, just ahead of the trigger guard. Although a few "underhammer" pieces had been made, they were never popular due to the difficulty of retaining the priming powder in the frizzen pan. There would be no such problem with the weapon in his hands. It did not have a frizzen pan, nor even a nipple to take a percussion cap. Another omission was a ramrod, and there was no provision made to carry what was normally an indispensable aid to reloading. However, the most noticeable departure from the standard "Kentucky's" fittings was a rectangular metal bar with rounded ends which passed through an aperture in the frame and a leverlike device behind it on the right side.

There was no need for Ole Devil to wonder what the weapon might be. It was his Browning Slide Repeating rifle, which had been in the leather boot—still something of an innovation—attached to the left side of the dun's saddle. What was more, as one of the three five-shot magazines that had been in a leather pouch on the back of his waistbelt was now positioned in the aperture on the piece's frame, the Mexican either knew, or had deduced, its purpose.

The other two magazines, Ole Devil's saber, and his matched pair of pistols—one of which was carried in a holster that, along with the sword, hung over his saddle horn—lay at his captor's feet.

"That's better, *señor,*" the Mexican remarked, taking his eyes from the weapon and looking at the Texian. "Are you sufficiently recovered to understand me?"

"Just about," Ole Devil admitted. "But I'm as uncomfortable as hell. Can I sit up, please?"

"If you wish," the Mexican authorized, with an air of friendly magnanimity, but he made no offer to help. Instead, he continued to study the rifle while the Texian shuffled laboriously to sit propped against the trunk of the tree. Then he went on, "This is a remarkable weapon—if it works."

"It works well enough," Ole Devil declared, puzzled by his captor's attitude and playing for time almost instinctively; although he did not know what good gaining it might do.

"Then it's a great pity that it will only fire five shots in succession," the Mexican remarked, cradling the butt against his shoulder and sighting along the forty and five-sixteenths of an inch-long octagonal barrel so that its .45-caliber muzzle was directed at the center of its owner's chest. "Of course, under certain conditions, *one* would be sufficient."

"When Jonathan Browning* saw how difficult it was to carry with the slide in place, he decided that five was the number that could be handled most conveniently," Ole Devil explained, noticing that the hammer had not been drawn down into the fully cocked position and guessing that his captor was merely playing a cat-and-mouse game with him. So he was able to show no concern and spoke as if making nothing more than casual conversation. "He'll make slides to take greater numbers as a special order."

"That's interesting," the Mexican said thoughtfully, his right forefinger caressing the trigger. Seeing no trace of alarm on his captive's face, he turned the barrel out of its alignment with an air of annoyance and disappointment. "Does he make many rifles like this?"

"I don't know," Ole Devil admitted, deciding against claiming that the majority of the Republic of Texas's Army were supplied with similar weapons. "It's the only one I've come across, but I expect he's made and sold more."†

---

*Jonathan Browning was the father and tutor of the master firearms' designer, John Moses Browning, who appears in CALAMITY SPELLS TROUBLE.

† Despite the difficulty of transporting it with the magazine in position, Jonathan Browning had produced a comparatively simple repeating rifle which was capable of a continuous fire unequaled by any contemporary

"I've never heard of a weapon like this," the Mexican stated. "An army equipped with them would be a formidable thing."

"Except that the generals would never accept anything so new," Ole Devil pointed out, wondering what the conversation was leading up to.

"That's true enough," the Mexican conceded and gave a shrug. Laying the rifle down carefully alongside the other weapons, he straightened with an attitude of being ready to get to business. "Enough of this small talk, *señor*. The time has come for us to introduce ourselves. I am Major Abrahan Phillipe Gonzales *de* Villena *y* Danvila, of the Arizona Hopi *Activos* Regiment, at your service."

The introduction accounted for the man being clad in a uniform with which Ole Devil was not acquainted. *Activos* were not members of the regular army, but reservists and local militia commanded by influential civilians from the districts in which they were raised. Coming from wealthy families, the majority of such officers selected whatever type of attire they fancied.

As, in general, the *Activos* regiments were formed of *peons* who were poorly trained, armed and equipped and who had little desire to become soldiers, they were not regarded as dangerous by the Texians. However, Ole Devil realized that his captors might prove to be an exception to the rule. Although the Hopi Indians, being a nation of settled pastoral agriculturalists, did not have a reputation as raiders and warriors like the Apaches, Yaquis and Comanches, they were

---

weapon. However, during the period when he was manufacturing it, between 1834–42, he lacked the facilities to go into large-scale production. He would have been able to do so in later years, but the development of self-contained metallic cartridges and more compact, if less simple, repeating arms had rendered it obsolete.

said to be tough and capable fighting men. So being a prisoner in their hands was not a thing to be taken lightly.

"May I ask who you are, *señor*?" Villena went on, when the Texian did not offer to respond to the introduction. "You will pardon me for doing so, but my curiosity has been aroused by meeting with a member of the Texas Light Cavalry in this part of the country—" He raised his hand in a mockingly prohibitive gesture as Ole Devil was about to speak. "Please, *señor, don't* try to deny it. I'm not one of those regular army clodhoppers. I've made a thorough study of—if you will excuse the use of the term—the enemy. The way you are dressed tells me that you serve in Colonel Edward Fog's '*regiment.*'"

"In that case, I won't deny it," the Texian promised, impressed by the extent of the Mexican's knowledge and hiding his annoyance over the note of derision with which the word "regiment" had been said.

"Then perhaps you will be good enough to answer my question," Villena suggested, still speaking politely, but the underlying threat in his voice was growing more noticeable.

"I decided that I didn't like the idea of being a soldier anymore," Ole Devil explained. "So I deserted."

"*You* are a deserter?" the Mexican purred, exuding disbelief and waving his hand almost languidly toward the weapons at his feet. "I very much doubt *that, señor.* A matched pair of percussion-fired pistols made by Joseph Manton of London, England, a 'bowie' knife inscribed with the name 'James Black, Little Rock, Arkansas,' a saber from L. Haiman and Brother, this remarkable rifle. They are not the arms supplied to an ordinary enlisted man. *You* are a *caballero,* like myself, *señor.* Men of our class do not desert."

Considering he was on dangerous ground, Ole Devil did not reply. Instead, he looked around the clearing again. He was no more fortunate than on the first occasion in finding something which might offer the slightest hope of escaping from his desperate situation. Certainly there was no help anywhere close at hand, unless the picket whom he had been on his way to visit—

"I must confess that I am puzzled, *señor,*" Villena stated, breaking into his captive's train of thought. "According to the information I was given, the Texas Light Cavalry are forming part of the screen for General Houston's flight. And yet I find *two* members of it over here near the coast."

Try as he might, Ole Devil could not prevent himself from giving some slight indication of how disturbing that news was. Yet, when he came to think of it, Villena had suggested that he had already met with another member of the Texas Light Cavalry. Which meant that he must have come across the picket. Even as Ole Devil regained control and halted the stiffening movement he was making, he knew that it had not gone unnoticed.

"Two of you, *señor,*" the Mexican confirmed, clearly delighted at having evoked even so small a response. "My scouts came upon the other at the edge of the woodland. But you know what these damned savages are like. Instead of taking him a prisoner, so that I could question him, one of them caved his skull in with a throwing stick."

The mocking timbre in the Mexican's voice filled Ole Devil with anger. Like any good officer, he took an interest in the men under his command. Although well qualified to handle the duty, having spent several years on the frontier, the picket was also a married man with two children. No matter how he had allowed the Hopis to come near enough to kill him, his death was a tragedy. However, the Texian controlled his emotions. Displaying them would serve no other purpose than to give amusement and pleasure to his sadistic captor.

"So you see my predicament, *señor,*" Villena went on, but he was clearly growing irritated by Ole Devil's continued refusal to respond to his goading. "My colonel has sent me on a scouting mission and I come across a member of the Texas Light Cavalry far from where he should be. But he is killed before I can question him. At first I tell myself he must be a deserter. Then I am told that one of his officers has been captured. So, being a man of intelligence, I ask myself, 'Why are they in *this* vicinity?' and find I cannot supply the answer."

Despite his distress over the death of the picket, Ole Devil was listening with growing relief. Up until then he had been afraid that, having learned about the consignment of caplocks, Santa Anna had sent a regiment to help the renegades who had tried to prevent their collection. Now he was sure that Villena's presence was no more than an unfortunate coincidence. In addition to the Mexicans' main force, which was marching toward San Antonio de Bexar, there were said to be two other columns on their way to invade Texas. In all probability, the Arizona Hopi *Activos* Regiment were the advance party from one of the latter.

"Perhaps *you* would care to supply me with the answer, *señor*?" Villena suggested. "I'd advise you to do so. These Indians of mine can be most brutal. Much as I would dislike to have to give the order, they'll make you talk whether you want to or not."

"I've nothing to say," Ole Devil replied.

"That is a foolish attitude, *señor*," Villena warned. "And one which will avail you nothing. Much as I would regret the necessity, my sense of duty would compel me to employ even barbarous and painful means if that is the only way in which I can get the information I require from you. Tell me what I want to know and I give you my word that I will set you free."

"You will?" Ole Devil gasped, with well-simulated eagerness.

"I will," Villena confirmed. "You have my word on it."

An experienced poker player, Ole Devil had become experienced at reading facial expressions. As the Mexican was giving the assurance, a malicious glint came to his eyes and his lips twisted into a derisive sneer. It was obvious to the Texian that his captor was still playing the cat-and-mouse game by making such an offer. Even if he supplied the information, it would not save him from torture and death. Yet he also had to concede that Villena was playing the game in a clever fashion. The pretended amiability and reluctance to employ painful methods was calculated to lessen his resistance when the latter were being applied.

"Is *your* word worth as much as that of General Cós?" Ole Devil inquired, dropping his former attitude and eyeing the Mexican in open derision.

Anger darkened Villena's features, wiping away every trace of amiability and showing that the thrust had gone home. He had had no intention of keeping his word, but had been convinced that the Texian believed he would do so. Knowing what was implied by the question,* he realized that he was wrong.

"Very well, *gringo!*" Villena spat out, dropping all his pretense. "We'll see how long you will refuse to talk." Looking over his shoulder, he barked in Spanish, "Many Plantings, make this one tell me everything I want to know. Do it slowly. I want to hear him scream and beg me to make you stop."

---

* On December 6, 1835, at the end of a battle lasting for six days, General Martin Perfecto de Cós and his force of eleven hundred men had surrendered to the Texians at San Antonio de Bexar. On Cós giving his parole that he and his men would refrain from further military action against the Republic of Texas, they were allowed to return unharmed to Mexico. As Cós was accompanying the army which was marching north, it was apparent that he did not intend to honor the terms of his parole.

4

I'LL MAKE SURE OF YOU!

Watching the five Hopi Indians standing up and starting to walk in his direction, Ole Devil Hardin stiffened slightly. No coward, he was also far from being a reckless fool. So he did not try to delude himself regarding the predicament he was in. Bound hand and foot, there was little enough he could do in his own defense. Nor could he expect any mercy from his captors. Even if he gave Major Abrahan Phillipe Gonzales *de* Villena *y* Danvila the required information, it would not save him.

Not that Ole Devil even considered taking such a course. He knew how much the consignment of caplock rifles could mean to the Army of the Republic of Texas in the struggle which was still to come. Yet he could also see one disadvantage in refusing to speak. Villena was already curious over having found two members of the Texas Light Cavalry so far from their regiment's recorded position. If he did not receive an answer of some kind, he was certain to investigate.

By going along the route taken by Ole Devil, who had not troubled to try and conceal his tracks, the Mexican would eventually arrive at Santa Cristóbal Bay. Of course there was a chance that one of the pickets visited by the Texian would not be taken by surprise and deliver a warning to Mannen Blaze. In that case, preparations could be made to protect the consignment. The snag to that was, while Villena was accompanied only by a small party, there was almost certain to be a larger force from the Arizona Hopi *Activos* Regiment not too far away. Even if the reinforcements were not sufficient in numbers to defeat Company "C," they could harass the mule train and at least slow down the delivery even if they were unable to stop it.

"Come on!" Villena commanded in Spanish, stepping back a few paces, his face ugly with sadistic anticipation. "Get to work on him!"

Understanding the Mexican's words, Ole Devil brought his thoughts on the situation to an end. The Hopi with the red headband snapped something in his own tongue. Darting forward, the two youngest of the other braves—who, like their companions, were advancing empty-handed—grabbed the Texian by the feet. Giving him no chance to resist, they dragged him away from the tree. Although he managed to avoid having his head banged against the trunk, he could do nothing to prevent himself from being hauled along the ground.

Releasing the boot he was grasping, the shorter of the braves drew his knife. Stepping into position, he dug the fingers of his other hand into Ole Devil's hair. With a savage jerk, he snatched the Texian into a sitting position. Searing pain which seemed to be setting the top of his skull on fire brought tears involuntarily to Ole Devil's eyes, but he managed to hold back the yelp of torment that the sensation almost caused. At any moment, he expected to feel the knife's blade biting into his flesh. It would not be a mortal thrust, but merely designed to hurt.

Sucking in a breath, Ole Devil prepared to resist any inclination to cry out. If possible, he meant to die well. However, before he did, he must give Villena some satisfactory yet untrue explanation for his presence. Not only would it have to be believable, but it would have to send the Mexican as far away as possible from Santa Cristóbal Bay and the route to be taken by the mule train.

The expected cut from the knife did not materialize!

Instead, there was a hissing sound which every man present recognized!

Even Ole Devil could hardly believe the evidence of his ears!

Passing between the other braves, having flown from among the bushes at the northern edge of the clearing, an arrow struck the Texian's assailant just below the left armpit. It arrived with such a velocity that the shaft sank in to the fletching and sent the stricken brave reeling. Spinning around helplessly on buckling legs, he measured his length on the ground.

Startled exclamations burst from the Mexican and the rest of the warriors. Swiveling around with hands grabbing for the *épée-de-combat*, knives, tomahawks, or—in the eldest brave's case—a pistol, Villena and the Hopis stared in the direction from which the arrow had come. What they saw was cause for concern and relief; particularly for those warriors who realized that they were some distance from weapons which offered a greater range than those they carried.

Only a single man was standing among the bushes. Small, bareheaded, clad in black garments, he did not look like a Texian. In fact he was unlike anybody, Indian, Mexican, or *gringo,* the Hopis had ever seen. Nor was Villena any better informed as to what nationality he might belong.

Experienced warriors, the Indians recognized one thing!

In spite of the newcomer's lack of inches—he was barely as

tall as the *mozo** holding Villena's *palomino* gelding—he could not be dismissed as harmless. In his left hand was—compared with his stature—a remarkably long bow, its handle set two thirds of the way down the stave instead of centrally. His stance for shooting appeared strange to the Indians' eyes,† but that clearly did not make it any the less effective. Already, moving with the smoothly flowing speed of a highly trained archer, his right hand was plucking another arrow from the quiver on his back.

"Get him, *pronto!*" Villena screeched furiously, starting to slide the *épée-de-combat* from its sheath.

Nocking the arrow to the string and laying its shaft on the shallow "V" formed by the base of his left thumb and the bow's stave, the newcomer made his draw with what appeared to be a circling motion of his arms.

The Hopi braves were starting to move forward without waiting for their Mexican superior's order. Although their people did not have the cult of the warrior so highly developed as in the nomadic nations who lived by hunting and raiding, they too were taught to regard a coup taken by personal contact as more estimable than making a kill from a distance. What was more, they considered that they would have a better chance of dealing with the diminutive foreigner at close quarters than by taking the time—brief as it would be—to go and retrieve their bows or throwing sticks. The speed with which he was moving warned them that every second's delay would be deadly dangerous.

Tugging to liberate the pistol which he had taken from the dead gringo's body, Chief Many Plantings became aware that he was in peril. He saw the little man's left index finger, which was extended instead of being coiled around the bow's

---

* *Mozo: a manservant, particularly one serving in a menial capacity.*
† *A description of Tommy Okasi's archery technique is given in* YOUNG OLE DEVIL

handle with its mates, pointing straight at him from just below the arrow. However, he refused to be deterred by the
discovery that he was selected as the next target. A warrior
who elected to carry a war lance was expected to set an example by having a complete disregard for his personal safety.
So he continued to step forward and, as the weapon came
free, his left hand went toward it with the intention of cocking the hammer. If he was to die, he would give his younger
companions—to the parents of whom he had a responsibility
for their welfare—an improved chance of survival.

Even as the chief was commencing his second stride, before his left hand could reach the pistol, the small man had
completed his draw and taken sight. Loosing his hold on the
string, he allowed the flexed limbs of the bow to return to
their original curves. Propelled across the intervening space
so swiftly that the eye could barely follow its movements, the
arrow reached its mark. The needle sharp, razor edged steel
point, set horizontally on the shaft, passed between Many
Plantings's left ribs and through his heart. He stumbled backward, dying as he would have wished, with a weapon in his
hand and facing an enemy.

"Kill the little devil!" Villena shrieked as the chief went
down, but he did not offer to go and help carry out his command.

Nor was the Mexican's exhortation needed by the remaining braves. The sight of their leader receiving a fatal wound
gave them an added inducement to reach and deal with the
man who had inflicted it. What was more, they felt sure that
they could make contact with him before he was able to take
out, nock, draw, and aim another arrow.

Obviously the newcomer shared the Hopi warriors' summation of the situation. He made no attempt to recharge his
bow. Instead, he tossed it aside. Having done so, his left hand
flashed upward at an angle. The quiver's shoulder strap was

joined together by a knot which disintegrated as he grasped
and tugged sharply at one protruding end. Having released
the quiver from restraint, he allowed it to fall behind him and
out of his way. Then he bounded rapidly toward the advancing trio.

Despite the small man's display of competence up to that
point, both in having reached his position without being detected and in the way he had handled the bow, his latest
actions appeared to be a serious error in tactics. Although a
pair of swords swung in sheaths from his waistbelt, he was
darting forward with empty hands to meet three larger,
heavier enemies—each of whom was already grasping a
weapon ready for use.

Still seated, as he had been since the Indian had dragged
him into that position by his hair, Ole Devil watched. He
recognized his rescuer and was far from perturbed at seeing
what Villena and the braves regarded as a fatal mistake on
the small newcomer's part. In fact, he had no doubt that it
was the three Hopis who were going to suffer for their over-
confidence and ignorance of the truth about the man they
were rushing to attack.

The ignorance was understandable, Ole Devil realized. At
that period, there were few people in the Western world who
would have anticipated Tommy Okasi's potential as a highly
skilled fighting man. The Chinese coolies and merchants—
and their number was far from extensive—with whom the
majority of Occidentals came into contact were, in general, a
passive race who rarely displayed any knowledge of armed,
or unarmed, combat.

However, Tommy was not Chinese.

Some five years earlier, the merchant ship commanded by
Ole Devil's father had come across a derelict Oriental vessel
drifting in the China Sea. Half dead from hunger and thirst,
Tommy had been the sole survivor. He had had no posses-

sions apart from the clothing on his back, his *daisho*,* a bow six foot in length and a quiver of arrows.

On recovering, it had been found that Tommy spoke a little English. When questioned, while he had described what had happened to the rest of the crew, he had not explained his reason for being aboard the stricken vessel. Nor had he evinced any desire to return to his as yet little known native land, Japan.† Instead, he had made a request to be allowed to stay on Captain Hardin's ship. When this had been granted, he had attached himself to his rescuer's son who had helped persuade Captain Hardin to keep the little Oriental.

Whatever had been the cause of Tommy's disinclination to go home, it had proved to be most beneficial as far as Ole Devil was concerned by providing him with a loyal and useful friend. Although Ole Devil did not acquire the proficiency of another—as yet unborn—member of the Hardin, Fog and Blaze clan,* he had learned a number of useful unarmed fighting tricks from the little Oriental. However, while highly adept in his nation's very effective martial arts, Tommy had insisted upon serving in the capacity of Ole Devil's valet.

In spite of his passive occupation, the little Oriental had never hesitated to participate in any hazardous activity upon which his employer had become engaged. Not only had he played an important part in Ole Devil's escape from jail in Crown Bayou, he had willingly joined in the missions carried out by his companions since their arrival in Texas. Tommy had helped Ole Devil to deal with the renegades who had

* Daisho: *a matched pair of swords, comprising of a* tachi *with a thirty-inch-long blade and a* wakizashi, *the blade of which was eighteen inches in length.*
† *Until the visits in 1853–54 of a flotilla commanded by Commodore Perry, U.S.N., there was little contact between the Western World and Japan.*
* *How Dustine Edward Marsden "Dusty" Fog made use of the tutelage which he received from Tommy Okasi is told in the author's "Civil War" and "Floating Outfit" stories.*

tried to prevent them reaching Santa Cristóbal Bay and had also done much to ensure that, having left, the Mexican warship which had been there would be unable to return.

So, all in all, Tommy Okasi was well able to take care of himself.

Nor was the little Oriental acting in as reckless a manner as it appeared to Villena and the Hopis.

Having saved Ole Devil from the knife of the first brave and dealt with the man whom he had calculated was posing the most immediate threat to himself, Tommy had realized that the affair was far from at an end. The rest of the Indians clearly intended to attack him and there was also the Mexican to be taken into consideration. So, thinking fast, he had decided how he could best deal with the situation. Having reached his conclusions, he did not waste time in putting them into practice. Going to meet the trio without holding a weapon was part of his plan, designed to lull them into a sense of false security.

Although they were trained warriors, the three Hopis had never come into contact with a man like Tommy. So they attached no greater thought to his apparently foolhardy behavior than to consider that it would make him an easy victim for whichever of them reached him first.

In their individual eagerness to be the one who counted coup, each brave was running at his best speed. Before they had covered half of the distance, they had attained a rough arrowhead formation with the youngest of them at its point. Waving his tomahawk over his head and whooping his delight, he charged onward. Still the strange looking little foreigner was showing no sign of arming himself. Nor was he slackening his pace. To the brave, it seemed that he intended to do neither but meant to come to grips with his bare hands. Having drawn his conclusion, the Hopi made ready to strike without bothering to guard himself against possible reprisals.

For all the seeming disregard of danger which Tommy was showing, he was calculating the distance between himself and the leading brave with great care and studying the relative positions of the other two. When he estimated that the time was right, he made his moves and they proved to be devastatingly effective.

One of the martial subjects in which the little Oriental had acquired considerable proficiency was *laijitsu*, fast sword drawing. Although he no longer carried his *daisho* in the manner of his forefathers,* he could still produce either of the weapons with remarkable speed.

Darting across in a flickering blur of motion, Tommy's right hand closed around the hilt of the *tachi* just above the three and three-eighths of an inch diameter circular *tsuba*, hand guard. Even as he was whipping the thirty-inch-long, reverse-Wharncliffe point† blade from its bamboo sheath, he weaved to his left. Nor did he act a moment too soon.

Launching a swing with sufficient power to sink the tomahawk deep into the top of its recipient's skull, the young brave was taken completely unawares by Tommy's change of direction. With a sensation of horror, he saw that his blow was going to miss. Then, just a fraction of a second too late, he realized that he was in terrible danger. However, there was neither the time nor the opportunity for him to take any evasive action.

"Kiai!" Tommy shouted, giving the traditional cry of self-

* *Traditionally, the* daisho *was carried through the girdle. However, as he had had to spend long periods on horseback since arriving in the United States, Tommy Okasi had found it was more convenient to equip the sheaths with slings which could be attached to his waist belt.*
† *Reverse-Wharncliffe point: where the cutting edge joins the back of the blade in a convex arc. The normal Wharncliffe, also called a "beak," point —said to have been developed by the Earl of Wharncliffe in the sixteenth century, although variations of it had been in use since Roman times—is mainly used on pocketknives and has the back of the blade making a convex arc to the cutting edge.*

assertion, as the sword came clear of the sheath and, making a glistening arc, continued to sweep around to the right.

Such was the little Oriental's skill at *laijitsu* that the *tachi* reached its destination before the brave's tomahawk-filled right hand had descended far enough to impede it.

The steel from which the *tachi* had been forged was as fine as could be found anywhere in the world. Produced by a master swordsmith with generations of experience behind him and involving techniques unknown outside of Japan,* its cutting edge had been ground and honed until it was as sharp as a barber's razor, but it was more pliant and far stronger. Nor had Tommy ever neglected it for it was still in the same excellent condition as it had been on the day it was presented to him by his father. So, in his hands, it was a weapon of terrifyingly lethal efficiency.

Just how lethal and efficient was soon evident.

Reaching the brave, even as his shocked mind was beginning to register the full horror of his predicament, the hardened cutting edge of the tachi's blade performed one of the functions for which it had been designed. Slitting into the unprotected region below the rib cage, it passed through as if the living tissues were incapable of offering any resistance. Having disemboweled him, it emerged and rose until its

---

* After the blade had been shaped by fusing together numerous layers of steel, it was ready to be tempered. A claylike material, for which every master swordsmith had his own secret recipe, was applied to the whole of the blade apart from an inch or so at the tip and the entire cutting edge. After heating the blade to the correct temperature—traditionally this was commenced in the half light of the early morning—it was plunged into a tub of cold water. The exposed metal cooled instantly and became very hard. Being encased in the clay sheath, the rest of the blade lost its heat gradually and, remaining comparatively soft, was given a greater pliancy. To prove that the finished article was capable of carrying out the work for which it was intended, the smith beat it against a sheet of iron and hacked to pieces the body of a dead criminal before handing it over to its owner. This is, of course, only a simplified description of the process.

point was directed away from the little Oriental. Releasing the tomahawk, the stricken brave's hands went to the wound in an unavailing attempt to close it. He blundered past his would-be victim on buckling legs, falling first to his knees and then face downward.

Having avoided being struck by his leading assailant, Tommy was confronting the remaining pair of braves. As he advanced so as to pass between them, his right fist rotated until its knuckles were pointing at the ground and the left hand went to the handle of the sword. Taking hold above its mate, it acted as a pivot for the other's leverage. Driving to the left with a similar deadly speed to that of the first blow, the blade met the side of the second brave's neck and sliced onward. The Hopi's head parted company with his shoulders, toppling to the ground as nervous reactions caused his decapitated body to continue its forward movement.

On the point of making an attack with his tomahawk, the last of the braves saw what was happening to his companion. The sheer horror of the sight, intensified by the fact that the havoc had been created by such a small man as Tommy, caused him to hesitate. Nor was he permitted to regain his wits.

Taking away his left hand and ignoring the headless Hopi, Tommy curled the *tachi* around in a half-circular motion. His right knuckles swiveled until they were upward and the weapon swept at its next target in a whiplike motion which no other type of sword could duplicate. Although only the last three inches of the blade made contact, they were sufficient. Passing under the brave's chin, the steel laid his throat open to the bone and he crumpled dying to the ground.

With the unsheathed *épée-de-combat* in his right hand, Villena was staring across the clearing. Although reluctant to believe his eyes, he accepted that they were not playing him false. When he saw the third of the braves being struck down, he realized that there was nobody left between himself and the strange, yet deadly, little foreigner. For all that, the Mexican believed he had one advantage over his subordinates. They had rushed recklessly into the attack on the assumption that the newcomer would be easy meat. Having seen how fatally wrong such deductions were, he had no intention of duplicating their mistakes. A skilled fencer, used to fighting against a man armed with a sword—which none of the Hopis had been—he was confident that he could more than hold his own.

Another thought struck Villena as he was reaching his conclusions regarding Tommy. From his actions, if not his attire and armament, it seemed likely that the small man was another member of the Texas Light Cavalry. It was possible that there were more of them close by and they could arrive before he was able to dispatch the little swordsman. In which case, he would be advised to withdraw if he wanted to stay alive and avoid capture.

However, Villena's every instinct told him that the uncommunicative Texian prisoner was more than a mere enlisted man and could be engaged upon a mission of importance. If that should be so, duty demanded that he must be prevented from carrying it out.

There was only one way to ensure that the Texian did not continue with whatever duty had brought him to the east of his regiment's reported position. Killing him would not only deprive the rebels of a capable fighting man, but would satisfy Villena's sadistic pleasure in inflicting pain.

"I'll make sure of you!"

Shouting the words, the Mexican sprang forward with the intention of killing his prisoner.

5
IF HE COMES, HE WON'T BE ALONE

Hearing the words yelled by Major Abrahan Phillipe Gonzales *de* Villena *y* Danvila, Ole Devil Hardin's attention was drawn from the brief fight that had taken place at the side of the clearing. Instantly he realized that his life was still in as great a danger as it had been prior to Tommy Okasi's fortunate arrival. With a good forty yards to cover, there was no hope of the little Oriental being able to reach them quickly enough to save him.

Having drawn a similar conclusion, the Mexican did not anticipate any difficulty in dispatching his prisoner. Seated on the ground, with his hands bound behind his back, and ankles lashed together, he was in no position to defend himself. So Villena went into a lunge, aiming the point of his *épée-de-combat* at the Texian's left breast.

Watching the needle-sharp point of the Toledo steel blade darting in his direction, Ole Devil was grateful for one thing. The conversation he had had with Villena had allowed him to clear his head. While he had not thrown off all the effects of being knocked unconscious when the Hopi Indian had dragged him from his saddle, his condition was much improved.

Thinking fast and taking into consideration that Tommy was already running toward them, Ole Devil decided that there was something he could do about his predicament. While it would be risky in the extreme, it offered him his only slender hope of salvation.

Waiting until Villena's sword was within inches of him, Ole Devil threw himself backward. So accurately had he timed the evasion that the weapon passed above him—but only just. Instead of piercing his heart, the point brushed the lobe of his left ear as it went by. While his shoulders were descending, he raised and bent his legs until his knees were above his chest.

The Mexican was expecting to meet with some resistance as his blade sank into flesh. When it did not, his momentum carried him onward and his torso was inclined forward. Up thrust the Texian's feet, taking him in the center of his chest. While Ole Devil was unable to exert his full power, he had no reason to despise the result of his efforts.

Shoved backward, Villena staggered and, in his determination to retain his balance, lost his hold on the sword. As soon as he felt the hilt leaving his grasp, he appreciated just how badly his situation had changed. He was unarmed against an assailant who was carrying an effective and deadly weapon. So he took the only course that was left to him. Putting aside any notion of trying to retrieve his *épée-de-combat,* or collecting one of the Texian's arms, he managed to turn and run to where the frightened-looking *mozo* was holding his *palomino* gelding.

Snatching the reins and knocking the youngster aside, Villena vaulted astride the *palomino.* A pair of pistols were hanging in holsters from his saddle horn, loaded and ready for use. However, even as he was reaching for one with his right hand, he glanced in the direction from which he had fled. What he saw caused him to change his mind about drawing the weapon.

Being a shrewd fighting man, Tommy was aware that the loss of the *épée-de-combat* did not mean the Mexican was completely unarmed or defenseless. In fact, he had seen the pair of pistols carried by the gelding and realized that they could be a potent factor in the continuation of the fight. So he did not offer to go any closer to Villena.

Instead, Tommy swerved to where Ole Devil's weapons were lying. He noticed that there was a magazine attached to the Browning Slide Repeating rifle and decided it would be most suitable for his needs. Dropping the *tachi*, he bent to scoop it up.

Cursing himself for having made the rifle ready for firing, Villena could appreciate how it changed the situation. While he did not know how skilled the little foreigner might be in the use of firearms, he was disinclined to taking the chance of finding out. A fair pistol shot, but not exceptional, he was sitting on a horse already made restless by his hurried and far from gentle arrival astride its back. So its movements were not making a steady base from which to take aim, particularly when he would be opposed by a man holding a weapon which had a greater potential so far as accuracy was concerned. Putting discretion before valor, the Mexican clapped his spurs against the gelding's flanks and set it into motion.

"Don't let him get away, Tommy!" Ole Devil commanded, but he was not acting out of a desire for revenge against his captor. "He knows too much!"

Swinging the butt of the rifle to his shoulder without acknowledging the order, the little Oriental took aim. His right forefinger drew down the underhammer to fully cocked and returned to the trigger. It tightened as the sights were aligned on the fleeing Mexican's back.

Although the hammer rose, nothing else happened!

Surprised, for the weapon had previously never misfired, Tommy stared at it.

"Work the lever!" Ole Devil instructed, glancing around and guessing what had gone wrong.

Although Villena had deduced enough to fit the magazine through the aperture, he had not completed the simple loading process. Thumbing down the lever on the right side of the frame set the mechanism into operation. Not only was the chamber aligned, it was cammed forward and held so that the face of the magazine formed a gas-tight connection against the bore of the barrel.

In his ignorance, the Mexican had saved his life.

Carrying out his employer's advice, Tommy manipulated the lever and felt the magazine move into position. However, by the time he had done so and pulled down the hammer again, Villena was approaching the edge of the clearing. For all that, before he could enter the woodland, the little Oriental had the rifle's barrel pointing at the center of his back. Satisfied that he was holding true, Tommy started to squeeze the trigger.

Having been knocked on to his rump by the force of his employer's shove, the *mozo* let out a wail of alarm as he realized that he was being deserted. The sound distracted Tommy at the worst possible moment, with the hammer just liberated from the sear. There was the crack of detonating black powder, but the muzzle had wavered out of alignment. He missed, but not by much.

In passing, the bullet snipped through one of the *quetzal*'s plumes which dangled from the top of Villena's busby. Before Tommy could go through the Browning's reloading process, brief as it might be in comparison with contemporary single-shot arms, the Mexican was urging the *palomino* to greater speed and was partially concealed among the trees.

"Get after him!" Ole Devil barked, appreciating how difficult trying to shoot the swiftly moving Villena would be under the circumstances.

"Best I set you free first," Tommy replied, lowering the rifle. "I don't think he will be turning back, but if he comes, he won't be alone."

Accepting the wisdom of the little Oriental's comment, Ole Devil did not argue. In fact, he was considerably relieved by the prospect of being released from his bonds. He realized that it was his earlier preoccupation with his private affairs which had resulted in him being taken prisoner, at a time when he should have been devoting his entire attention to the needs of the Republic of Texas. The thought was far from pleasing. It was, he told himself grimly, the first time he had made such an error for that reason and he promised himself it would be the last.

Setting down the Browning rifle, after a glance to make sure that the wailing and still seated *mozo* was not planning to take any hostile action, Tommy drew his *wakizashi*. Bending, he used its eighteen-inch-long, razor-sharp blade to sever the rawhide thongs holding Ole Devil's ankles. Then, stepping behind his employer, he liberated the wrists.

"*Gracias!*" Ole Devil gritted, trying to conceal the pain which the renewal of his impeded circulation was causing. "How the hell did you come to be here so conveniently when I needed you?"

"Old Nipponese saying—" Tommy began.

"Which you've just made up," Ole Devil put in through clenched lips, making what had become an accepted response to such a statement by the little Oriental.

"Man with great personal problem on his mind less capable of taking care of himself," Tommy went on, as if the interruption had never taken place, returning the *wakizashi* to its sheath. There was, although he would not have admitted it, complete justification for his employer's comment and he continued, "So Di and Mannen-san sent humble and unworthy self to watch over you."

"Why that was right neighborly and considerate of you, I'm sure," Ole Devil declared and thrust himself to his feet. "And thank you 'most to death. Come on, I want to find out what happened to Ilkey."

"I already have," Tommy replied, as the Texian went toward his weapons. "That's why I didn't get here sooner. I didn't want you to know I was following, so I wasn't too close and I lost sight of you. So I went straight to where we'd left Ilkey. When I found his body and you weren't there, I came looking for you. I heard you talking and moved in on foot."

While the little Oriental was speaking, Ole Devil picked up one of the Manton pistols. After checking that it had not been tampered with and was still capable of being fired, he thrust its barrel through the loop on his belt. Then he retrieved the bowie knife and slid its eleven inches long, two and a quarter inches wide, three-eights of an inch thick clip point blade* into the sheath. Collecting the rifle's two spare magazines, he returned them to the pouch on the back of his belt. By the time he had done so, Tommy was holding the second pistol and the saber.

"Are there any more of them around?" Tommy inquired, nodding toward the dead Indians.

"I'd say 'yes' to that," Ole Devil replied and picked up his rifle. "Let's find out how many and how near they are."

Although the *mozo* was no longer wailing, he had not attempted to rise. Instead, he had remained crouching on the ground, hoping to avoid drawing attention to himself. He stared in horror as the two men began to walk in his direc-

---

* Clip point: where the back of the blade curves to meet the main cutting edge in a concave arc five and a quarter inches in length. It is sharpened and forms an extension of the cutting edge.

tion. Nor could he decide which was the more frightening. The smaller had killed Many Plantings and the other Hopi braves, three of them with his sword, taking one's head off with a single blow. However, despite having seen the taller as a bound and helpless prisoner, his appearance aroused a sense of superstitious dread in the youngster. His hair and face made him look like the pictures of *el Diablo*, the Devil, which the *mozo* had been shown many times by the fathers at his local mission.

"Have mercy, *señores*," the youngster screeched in Spanish, crossing himself with great vigor. "It wasn't me who attacked you. I had to come with my *patrón* to—"

"Don't be frightened," Ole Devil put in gently, employing the same language. "We won't harm you if you answer our questions truthfully."

"Wh—What do you want to know, *señor*?" the *mozo* whimpered, gazing up as the two young men halted before him.

"Where are the rest of your regiment?" Ole Devil asked.

"F—Far off, *señor*," the youngster replied, waving his right hand vaguely to the southwest. "D—Don Abrahan left the camp early yesterday morning and we've been traveling ever since."

"How many more men did he have with him?"

"N—None, *señor*."

"*None?*" Ole Devil challenged.

"None, *señor*," the *mozo* confirmed. "I was told that the rest of the regiment were staying where they are until we returned and then it would be decided which way we will march. I hope that it is back home."

"I think he's speaking the truth," Ole Devil stated, having reverted to English so that he could translate the conversation for his companion's benefit. "In which case, we've some time in hand to get the consignment on the move."

"Do the Mexicans know about it?" Tommy inquired.

"Not from the way that Villena spoke when he was questioning me."

"Then he might not come back."

"I don't intend to count on it," Ole Devil declared. "He was no fool and finding members of the Texas Light Cavalry this far east aroused his curiosity. So he could persuade his colonel that investigating things might be worthwhile."

"How many men do they have?" Tommy wanted to know.

"He can't say for sure," Ole Devil replied, after putting further questions to the *mozo*. "Over a hundred, but only a few of them have firearms."

"Even with that few, they still have us outnumbered," Tommy pointed out. "And they can travel faster than we'll be doing with the mule train."

"That's for sure," Ole Devil agreed. "So the more miles we can put between us and them, the better I'll like it. I'll go back to the bay and tell Di what's happened. Keep watch here until I send a couple of men to relieve you."

"What about him?" Tommy asked, indicating the *mozo*.

"We'd better keep him with us for the time being," Ole Devil decided. "Let him bury Ilkey and fetch him in with you when you're relieved."

"I'll see to it," Tommy promised. "Are you all right?"

"It's mainly my pride that's hurt," Ole Devil admitted wryly. "Shall I leave you my rifle?"

"I'd rather rely on my bow," Tommy replied and his next words were more of a statement than a question. "We won't be going back to Crown Bayou?"

"No," Ole Devil answered quietly, removing the magazine from his rifle and returning it to the vacant space in the pouch. "We won't be going back. Provided we can hold on to it, Texas's our home from now on."

"I'll go and fetch my horse before you leave," Tommy suggested, guessing what reaching such a decision must have cost his employer and refraining from further discussion.

"That'd be advisable," Ole Devil agreed, knowing that the little Oriental might have need of the animal.

While waiting for his companion to return with his horse, Ole Devil made preparations for his own departure. Going to the horses, he discovered—as he had suspected—that the one he had not been able to see clearly earlier belonged to the dead picket. He examined his linebacked dun gelding to ensure that it had not been injured when he was dragged from its back. Satisfied that it had not, he slid the rifle into the saddle boot. Then he replaced the second pistol and saber in the holster and scabbard which were suspended on either side of the rig's low horn. All the time he was working, he kept the *mozo* under observation and was watched fearfully in return.

Telling the youngster to fetch his hat, which lay under the tree where it had fallen, Ole Devil donned it. Retrieving the pistol dropped by the chief of the Hopis, he took it to the picket's horse and tucked it into the bedroll on the cantle of the saddle. When an opportunity presented itself, he intended to send the animal and property to Ilkey's widow.

"I'll take Ilkey's horse with me and ride relay," Ole Devil announced, when Tommy joined him leading a powerful roan gelding and carrying the long bow and quiver of arrows. "You and the *mozo* there can bring the Hopis' mounts when you come. And don't take any chances. If the Mexican shows up with reinforcements, get away fast."

"I will," Tommy promised. "And you be watchful."

"Count on it," Ole Devil replied. "I don't make the same mistake twice."

"Old Nipponese saying, which I've just made up," Tommy said. "Wise man does not make the same mistake *once*."

"I'll keep it in mind for the future," Ole Devil promised

and, telling the *mozo* what was expected of him, swung astride the dun. Taking the reins of Ilkey's mount, which the little Oriental handed to him, he went on, "I'll see you back at the bay, Tommy."

Holding his mount at a steady trot, with the other horse following obediently as it had been trained to do, the Texian guided them into the woodland. He had decided against alerting the rest of his pickets by returning over the route he had taken on the outward journey. If the *mozo* had told the truth—and Ole Devil felt sure that he had been too frightened to lie—there was no immediate danger from the Arizona Hopi *Activos* Regiment. So he considered that he would be more usefully employed in rejoining his companions at Santa Cristóbal Bay with the minimum of delay.

Although Ole Devil was still disturbed by the news he had received via Beauregard Rassendyll and his decision regarding the future, he remembered the result of having become engrossed in his thoughts and he pushed the matter resolutely to the back of his mind. So he was far more alert than he had been on his way out from the bay. He saw nothing to disturb him, but did not regret his vigilance.

On his arrival, Ole Devil found that a considerable amount of work had already been completed. Not that he had expected anything else. For all Mannen Blaze's appearance of being half asleep, he was a reliable subordinate and could be counted upon to keep the men at any work to which they were assigned.

All of the consignment was on the beach and, from what Ole Devil could see, the vessel which had delivered it was already being made ready to leave. Looking around, he noticed that the oblong boxes were missing. The rifles were split into bundles of twelve and were being wrapped in pieces of sailcloth under Diamond-Hitch Brindley's supervision. Fortunately, the paper cartridges and percussion caps were in containers of a suitable size to be carried on the mules and did not require repacking.

"That looks like one of our boys' horses, Cousin Devil," Mannen remarked, indicating the animal alongside the dun as he, Di and Rassendyll came to meet the Texian.

"It was Ilkey's," Ole Devil replied and swung from the saddle.

"*Was* Ilkey's?" Mannen prompted.

"He's dead," Ole Devil said and explained what had happened.

"Hopis, huh?" Di growled at the end of the narrative. "I've never had any doings with 'em, but from what I've heard tell, they're tolerable tough *hombres*. Anyway, even if they come, we ought to be long gone by the time they get here."

"We'd better be," Ole Devil warned. "They'll have us outnumbered."

"Only we'll have 'em outgunned," Di pointed out. "Say one thing, though. It's right lucky for us all that we let ole Tommy go after you, Devil."

"Couldn't rightly figure any way to stop him once he got to figuring on doing it," Mannen supplemented indolently. "You know how he is. He's mighty set in his ways."

"Could be he had help to decide on following me," Ole Devil drawled, eyeing the girl and his cousin sardonically. Then he jerked his left thumb in the direction of the brig and went on, "Captain Adams isn't wasting any time in getting under way."

"We can't blame him for *that*," Rassendyll pointed out, studying the Texian without learning anything from the Mephistophelian features and wondering why the news he had brought had not produced the response he had anticipated. It almost seemed that Ole Devil was more distressed and perturbed than delighted in learning that his name was

cleared and that he was free to go back to Louisiana. However, there were matters of more pressing importance to be
taken care of. "I've let him take the rifle boxes for firewood."

"We'd only have had to burn them ourselves if you
hadn't," Ole Devil answered.

"Riders coming, Cap'n Hardin!" called the nearest of the
watchers posted on the top of the slope. "It looks like the
rest of our boys headed back."

"What the—?" Di exclaimed, for the report implied that
the riders were returning alone.

"Come on!" Ole Devil interrupted, having drawn a similar
conclusion, mounting the dun.

Darting forward, Di just beat Mannen Blaze to the dead
picket's mount. Like the burly Texian, she had removed her
horse's saddle. By appropriating Ilkey's animal, she was able
to accompany Ole Devil. They ascended the slope swiftly
and, on reaching the top, she found that her assumption had
been correct. Although the approaching riders were the remainder of Company "C," there was no sign of her grandfather and the mule train.

"Howdy, Di, Cap'n Hardin," greeted the lanky sergeant,
after looking around, as the two riders converged with his
party. "Seems like them two fellers was wrong."

"Which two fellers?" Di inquired.

"They met up with us on the trail," the sergeant elaborated. "Allowed they seed a fair-sized bunch of *hombres* led
by a right fine-looking, but somewhat mussed-up woman
headed this way."

"That sounds like that blasted de Moreau bitch and her
renegades, Devil," Di spat out.

"Which's what your grandpappy figured," the sergeant admitted. "So he told us to head back here and find out if you
needed a hand. Reckoned us coming up from behind, we'd
get 'em boxed in and whup 'em good."

"It's a pity they never came," Di declared. "We could have settled—"

"Turn your men, Sergeant!" Ole Devil barked.

"What's up?" Di asked, startled by the vehemence with which the order had been given.

"They haven't come here," Ole Devil replied. "So it must have been a trick to draw off the escort and let them attack the mule train. If they can stop it, they'll have us pinned down here until they can raise enough help to come and take the consignment from us."

6

THEY WON'T MOVE WITHOUT HER

Although Ole Devil Hardin was extremely perturbed by the thought that Ewart Brindley might have been tricked, he also realized that he could not set off immediately to satisfy himself upon the matter. First, taking into consideration the other development which had arisen to threaten the safety of the consignment, he had to organize additional protection for it. There was a chance that the *mozo* had been lying, or was mistaken, and the Arizona Hopi *Activos* Regiment could be much closer than he had claimed. So the circle of pickets had to be reinforced, thereby lessening the possibility of another lone man suffering the same fate as Ilkey; or, worse still, falling alive into the enemies' hands and being made to answer their questions. Unfortunately, the only way in which the pickets could be strengthened was by reducing the already small force who were at Santa Cristóbal Bay.

Under different circumstances, the arrival of Sergeant Maxime and his detail would have been a blessing. However, with the possible danger to the mule train, Ole Devil did not dare take the chance of adding the newcomers to his defenders. Instead, he told them to return as quickly as possible while he rejoined the rest of Company "C" and, after he had made his arrangements, he would follow.

Appreciating the difficulty the young Texian was having in deciding upon the best line of action, Diamond-Hitch Brindley did not attempt to influence him. Despite being aware of how tough her grandfather and his men were, she shared Ole Devil's concern for the safety of the consignment. However, she also knew that mentioning the matter would do nothing to lessen the burden of his responsibility.

"Shucks, Devil," the girl remarked, turning her borrowed mount at the Texian's side as Sergeant Maxime led the detail in the direction from which they had come. "Grandpappy Ewart's been taking good care of his-self for a heap of years. And I reckon him 'n' our Tejas packers can look out for themselves until your boys get back. Anyway, de Moreau don't have all that many men with her."

"That's the thing I'm counting on most," Ole Devil replied. "But, if she sent those men to tell your grandfather about seeing her and her men coming this way, she must have had a reason for doing it. I wish I could think what it was."

Throughout the short ride back to his waiting companions, the Texian tried to console himself with the thought that Di's final comment had been valid. The arrival of Mannen Blaze and Company "C" the previous day had scattered the renegades who were with Madeline de Moreau. Nor, even if she had managed to gather them again, were there so many as to have a great numerical supremacy over Brindley and his Tejas Indian employees.

In spite of the latter point, Ole Devil could not dispel his perturbation. He felt sure that the two men who had met the mule train were acting under Madeline de Moreau's orders. In which case, she must have had a good reason for sending them. Nothing he had seen of her led him to assume she was foolish. In fact, he had found her to be intelligent and un-scrupulous. So, if he was correct in his assumptions, she was planning mischief of some kind. He wished that he could guess what it might be.

Swinging from the dun's saddle near to the other horses, Ole Devil put aside his speculations so as to give his instructions to his cousin and Beauregard Rassendyll. Each picket was to be given a companion and warned about the Hopis, with orders to report to the bay immediately if any of them were seen. Fifty of the new caplocks were to be cleaned—all were coated in grease—ready for use and would be loaded as soon as word was received that the Indians were coming.

"I'll see to it," Mannen promised, after his cousin had explained the reason why he was being left in command. "And I've got something that will help. Uncle Ben Blaze sent me a Browning and three slides."

"That could come in handy all right," Ole Devil admitted. "But I hope that you don't need it."

"Tell you though," Di went on. "You might not be able to stop them Hopis a-coming, but with the caplocks and your lil ole Browning, you ought to be able to make 'em limp a mite going back."

"Like Cousin Devil says," Mannen drawled, his tones suggesting that he was having difficulty in staying awake, "I hope it doesn't come to that."

While the conversation had been taking place, Ole Devil was transferring his saddle and bridle to the big, powerful black gelding which was his second mount. Being fresh, it would travel at a better speed than the dun. As Di was equally aware of the need to move fast, she had been making her sorrel gelding ready instead of relying upon the mount belonging to the dead picket.

Satisfied that he had done all he could to safeguard the consignment and confident he could rely upon Mannen to do everything necessary, Ole Devil set off with the girl. They made good time, but the sun was going down before they arrived at their destination.

Topping a ridge which gave them their first view of the mule train, Di and the Texian could sense that their fears had been justified. The animals, still saddled and under the watchful gaze of the Tejas Indian packers, were standing in a bunch just beyond some bushes on the bank of a small stream. Forming a rough circle around them were a number of the Texian soldiers, positioned as if waiting to repel an attack. However, only half of Maxime's detail were present. Nor was there any sign of Brindley and his *cargador.** A further suggestion that something had happened was given by a gray horse which lay unmoving on its side a short way from the other animals. The sight of it brought a furious exclamation from the girl.

"Hell's teeth!" Di bellowed, reining in the sorrel. "Something's happened to ole Whitey!"

The words were directed at Ole Devil's back. Disturbed by what he was seeing, he signaled with his hands and heels for the black gelding to increase its pace. Nor, despite the shock she had received and appreciating what the loss of the white horse could mean, did the girl delay. Even as she stopped speaking, she urged her mount forward at a better speed and followed her grim-faced companion. Galloping across the intervening distance, they were almost neck and neck as they passed between two members of his company.

"Go in there, Cap'n Hardin!" called one of the soldiers, pointing toward the bushes.

Acting upon the somewhat inadequate advice, with the girl still at his side, Ole Devil went in the direction indicated by the man. Before they had gone many feet, he began to get an

* Cargador: *assistant pack master and second-in-command of a mule train.*

inkling of what the soldier had meant. At least two other members of his company were partially concealed by the foliage and it was impossible to tell what they were doing. Recognizing one as possessing a reasonable knowledge of medical and surgical matters, he felt an ever growing sense of alarm.

Sliding the black to a halt on the edge of the bushes, Ole Devil was quitting the saddle and allowing the reins to fall free even before it was fully at a stop. Responding with an equal alacrity, Di dismounted and accompanied him as he advanced on foot.

"Grandpappy!" the girl shrieked, as she and the Texian passed between some of the bushes to enter a small patch of open ground. "Joe!"

Ewart Brindley was lying on his back. About the same height as his granddaughter, he made up in breadth what he lacked in height. Stripped to the waist, his buckskin shirt having been cut off so that "Doc" Kimberley could get at the wound in the right side of his chest, he was well muscled and looked as hard and fit as a much younger man. Almost bald, with what little hair that remained a grizzled white, his leathery and sun-reddened features showed that, although he was trying to hide it, he was in considerable pain. He had on buckskin trousers, encircled by a belt with a big knife in an Indian sheath, and moccasins which extended to just below the knee.

Not far away, propped in a sitting position against the bent leg of a kneeling soldier, Brindley's *cargador* was having what appeared to be a wound on his forehead bandaged. About twenty years of age, Joe Galton was tall, red haired, good looking in a freckled and, usually, cheerful way. He wore buckskins and carried a knife on his belt.

To give her full credit, regardless of the discovery she had just made, Di did not go into a display of hysteria. Raised by her grandfather in a predominantly male society since her parents had been killed during her early childhood, she had seen much of life—and death. So she was able to restrain her external emotions after the initial reaction. Going forward, her body trembling slightly with the strain of acting in an impassive manner, she watched the tall, lean, unshaven, yet clean looking soldier who was attending to Brindley. Deciding that he was competent to handle the task, she halted and looked down. However, when she tried to speak, the question she wanted to ask would not come.

"How is he, Doc?" Ole Devil inquired, having moved forward and stopped at the girl's side. His left hand gave her right bicep a gentle squeeze of encouragement.

"He'll pull through, but it's bad enough to keep him off his feet for a while," Kimberley answered, in the accent of a well-educated Englishman, without taking his attention from his work. "Joe's got a bad graze on his forehead. The bullet just touched and glanced off. It knocked him from his horse and stunned him, but he was lucky. Another inch, or less— Lie still, sir."

The last words were directed at Brindley. Having opened his eyes, the old man was stirring and tried to sit up.

"Goddamn it!" Brindley gritted, as Kimberley enforced the request by pushing at his shoulders. "Get your cotton-picking hands offen—"

"You hush your mouth and do like he says, blast it!" Di yelped, springing forward and dropping to her knees at the other side of her grandfather. Spitting the words out almost breathlessly in her anxiety, she continued, "This gent knows what he's about and there's nothing you can do yet a-whiles."

"That's better," Kimberley went on, when his patient subsided more from agony-induced weakness than through any desire to be cooperative. He indicated a bulky, open saddlebag by his side, "I've got something in here will ease the pain."

"N—No—drugs for me!" Brindley protested feebly and managed to focus his eyes upon his granddaughter. "Damn it, Di-gal, they shot ole Whitey—"

"I saw," the girl admitted bitterly.

"Y—You—kn—know—what—that means?" the old man demanded.

"If I don't, you've sure as hell wasted a heap of time raising me," Di replied. "Which you haven't. So you just lie still while I go tend to things."

"Lemme come and—" Galton put in.

"I don't reckon you'd be a whole heap of help right now," Di answered, looking at the speaker. "So stay put, blast you. Ain't nothing you can do that I can't, not's needs tending to right now anyway. I'll see to things and the boys'll tell me what's happened."

"Hell, I'm not hurt all that bad!" the *cargador* objected, but his voice lacked conviction and his attempt to force himself away from the support given by the soldier's knee achieved nothing. Giving a low groan, he sank down again and raised a hand to his head. Trying to speak lightly, he went on, "I feel like I've just woke up after a night at Mama Rosa's *cantina.* So I wouldn't be a heap of help. Damned if you wasn't right, Di-gal."

"*I* never figured's I wasn't," the girl pointed out, returning her attention to Brindley and wagging her right forefinger in front of his face. "You do what the doc here says, mind. And that goes for you, Joe Galton." Having delivered her instructions, she looked at Kimberley and continued in milder tones, "Happen this pair of worthless goats give you any trouble, Doc, treat 'em like I do when they make fuss for me."

"How would that be, young lady?" the Englishman inquired, removing some of the contents from his saddlebag.

"Same thing's I do with the mules, which there's not a whole heap of difference 'tween 'em," Di elaborated. "Whomp 'em over the head with something heavy and's won't matter happen it gets busted."

"By jove! That strikes me as being a sound piece of medical advice," Kimberley declared, darting a glance filled with approbation at the girl. He could sense the deep emotional stress that she was experiencing and felt admiration for the way in which she kept it under control.

"Like they say," Di replied, straightening up. "You can do most anything with kindness, 'less you're dealing with mules —or men." Her gaze swung to Ole Devil. "You fixing to stand here jawing for the rest of the day?"

"It's a thought," the Texian answered. "But I wouldn't get any peace from you if I did, so I'll go and do some work."

"And not before time," Di sniffed.

"I don't know why he left England," Ole Devil remarked to the girl as they were walking through the bushes. "But he's a damned good doctor."

"I could see that, or you'd have heard me yelling," the girl stated and glared at the dead horse. "Goddamn it, Devil, if—"

"I'll be talking to Maxime about coming away from the train," Ole Devil promised and, in spite of the gentle way that he was speaking, his face became even more Satanic.

"It wasn't *his* fault, damn it," Di protested, realizing that her comment had been misinterpreted and her sense of fair play demanded that the error must be corrected. "You put those boys you sent under Grandpappy Ewart's orders and it was him, not ole Charlie Maxime's said they should head back to the bay and try to trap the renegades a-'tween us."

"Yes," Ole Devil conceded. "But—"

"There's no son-of-a-bitching 'but' about it!" the girl interrupted. "What in hell's use is it you giving a feller orders to take orders from somebody, then expecting him to pick and choose which of 'em he takes?"

"You're right," Ole Devil admitted, his lips twitching into a smile that he did not feel like giving. Again he gave Di's arm a gentle squeeze, for he shared Kimberley's feelings about her. "And saying what should have been, or laying blame, isn't going to change what happened. It's how we're affected and what's going to need doing now that counts. First, though, we better find out how it came about." He raised his voice, "Corporal Anchor!"

"Yo!" responded a medium-size and thickset soldier, rising and ambling swiftly toward his superior.

"What happened?" Ole Devil inquired, acknowledging the other's salute.

"I don't know, Cap'n," Anchor replied. "We heard shooting's we was coming back. But by the time we came into sight, it was all over. Ewart and young Joe Galton were down and the fellers who'd done it had lit out like the devil after a yearling. So Charlie Maxime sent me with Doc Kimberley and half of the boys to stand guard, then went after 'em with the rest."

While the brief conversation was taking place, a tall, well-made and middle-aged Tejas Indian approached from where he and his companions were attending to the mules. Dressed in buckskins and knee-high moccasins like the rest of the mule packers, he had on a high-crowned, wide-brimmed black hat with an eagle's tail feather in its band. He was armed with a big knife on his belt and had a "Plains" rifle across the crook of his left arm. There was something dignified and commanding about him and he showed none of the servility or debauchery which characterized many of his tribe

who lived and worked in close contact with Mexicans or Anglo-Saxon colonists.

The same applied to all of Brindley's Indian employees,
even Waldo, the aged cook, who occasionally went on a
drinking spree. All had avoided the "civilizing" influence of
the missions. Tough, hardy and capable, the old man, his
granddaughter and *cargador* treated them with respect and
they reciprocated by being loyal and hardworking.

"How Ewart 'n' Joe?" the man asked in a guttural voice. "I
see white feller know what him doing and tell him take them
in bushes in case bad *hombres* come back."

"They will both be all right," Di answered, speaking Tejas
fluently. "What happened, Tom?"

"We were tricked," replied Tom Wolf, the chief of the
mule packers, reverting to his native tongue.

"Tell me about it, please," the girl requested.

Keeping his face impassive, but speaking with a vehemence that was obvious to Ole Devil even though he did not
understand the language, Tom Wolf complied. He could
speak passable English, but felt—as did Di—that he could
make a more thorough explanation in his own tongue. So Di
listened and translated for the young Texian's benefit.

According to Tom Wolf, Sergeant Maxime had not been to
blame for leaving the mule train. The non-com had been
reluctant to do so, but Brindley insisted. On the face of it, the
decision had been correct; or at least justifiable under the
circumstances as they had known them. There was nothing
suspicious about the way that the two strangers had divulged
their information. In fact, it had come up in what seemed a
natural manner. They claimed to have seen a woman, who
looked to have been in a fight, leading a group of men to-
wards the coast. Not having cared for the appearance of the
party, they had kept out of sight and made their examination
with the aid of a telescope. On coming into view of the train,

they had concluded that—as its escort were soldiers—they would be advised to ride over and give a warning. They were, they had said, on their way west to join Houston and the Republic of Texas's Army.

Although Brindley had dispatched his military escort, in the hope of trapping the renegades, he did not accept his informants at face value. After they had ridden away, he told Tom Wolf to follow them. If they were working in cahoots with the woman and her band, such a possibility had been anticipated. Certainly they had neither turned back nor acted in a suspicious fashion up to the time that the sound of shooting from the rear had caused the Tejas chief to give up his observation and return.

Like the soldiers, Tom Wolf had arrived too late to participate in the fighting. Nor, much as he had wished to do so, was he able to go after his employer's assailants. Instead, he had remained with the mules and left the other task to Sergeant Maxime. In addition to attending to his duties, he had learned how the attack had taken place. The mule train was approaching the stream when a packer had seen a number of riders on a rim about half a mile to the south.

While the newcomers had behaved in a menacing fashion, they were only acting as a diversion. Four of their number had been concealed in a grove of post oaks less than a quarter of a mile to the north. As the exposed group approached, but before they had come into range of the defenders' weapons, the hidden men opened fire to hit Brindley, the *cargador* and the gray mare. Having done so, they withdrew and the threat of a charge, which was not launched, by their companions prevented the packers from giving chase.

"The men would have gone after them when the others rode away, but I stopped them," Tom Wolf concluded. "I could see the soldiers coming and knew we must look after Ewart, Joe and the mules."

"You acted with wisdom, Chief," declared Ole Devil, to whom the words had been directed in English. "I don't doubt the courage of your braves, or that you would have preferred to avenge the shooting of your friends."

"Do you want us to make camp here, Di?" asked the Indian, but the girl could see he was appreciative of and relieved by the young Texian's statement.

"It's all we can do." Di sighed, anger clouding her expressive face. After Tom Wolf had turned to go and give the necessary orders, she swung toward Ole Devil. "Goddamn it, even though they didn't scatter the mules like they was hoping, they couldn't have done worse to us than they did."

"They did just what they meant to do," the Texian answered.

"You mean all they was fixing to do was down Grandpappy Ewart and Joe?" the girl demanded.

"That was the idea, but they were told to shoot the bell mare as well," Ole Devil replied. "Whoever planned the ambush must have been around mules enough to know that, especially with a well trained team like this, they'd bunch and balk, but wouldn't scatter under fire, particularly with old Whitey down. From what you've told me, they won't move without her to lead them."

"They won't," Di confirmed, realizing what her companion was driving at.

Being hybrids, resulting from the crossing of a male donkey with a female horse, mules were only rarely capable of breeding. For all that, they tended to find the company of a mare irresistible. It was a trait which packers, handling large numbers of the animals, turned to their advantage. The mules would follow a mare all day without needing to be fastened together and, apparently soothed by a bell fastened around her neck, were content to remain close to her all night instead of requiring tying when on the trail.

"So, by dropping her, they've prevented us from collecting the consignment," Ole Devil continued. "There weren't enough of the renegades to tackle the train, especially if their *amigos* didn't manage to persuade at least part of the escort to leave it. Even with all of Sergeant Maxime's detail headed for the bay, they wouldn't be willing to risk their lives making a straightforward attack. They're fighting for what they can get out of it, not because of patriotism, and wouldn't take too many chances. I'll say one thing, though, Madeline de Moreau must be *very* persuasive to get them to do as much as they did."

"I'll 'persuasive' her if I get my hands on her!" Di spat out, with such pent-up fury that Ole Devil began to have a greater appreciation of just how great a strain she was under. Then, with a visible effort, she regained control of her emotions and her voice became almost normal as she continued, "What do you reckon she aims to do now she's got us stopped?"

"Either she's got more of her own band coming to attack us, or she's going to look for help from the Mexican Army to do it," Ole Devil guessed. "She's hoping that with your grandfather, Joe and the bell mare dead—or so she assumes —we'll not be able to move before she can get reinforcements."

"Which we won't," Di warned, "unless we can replace ole Whitey."

"Will the mules accept another mare?" Ole Devil asked.

"Shucks, yes. Just so long as she's got a bell on, they'll follow her. Do any of your boys ride a mare?"

"I'm afraid not. We've only geldings."

"That figures." Di sighed, being aware that having a mixed bunch of horses created problems which a military unit would wish to avoid.

"The nearest place we might find one is San Phillipe," Ole Devil remarked.

"Sure," the girl agreed, but showed a noticeable lack of enthusiasm. "You know the kind of folks who live there?"

"I do," Ole Devil admitted and his tone proved that he understood the cause of the girl's reaction. "They're just about as bad a bunch of cutthroats as can be found in Texas. But they're the quickest chance we have of laying hands on a mare. And without one, we'll never be able to move the consignment."

7

WE'LL BE ALL RIGHT—I
HOPE!

Accompanied by Diamond-Hitch Brindley and Tommy
Okasi, Ole Devil Hardin was traveling through the darkness
toward the cluster of lights and the various sounds which
marked the locations of the fifty or so dwellings and business
premises that comprised the town of San Phillipe. They rode
in line abreast, with the girl in the center, their attitudes
suggestive of extreme wary alertness. She and the Texian
were nursing their rifles, fully cocked and, in the latter's case,
with a five-shot slide magazine in the frame. The little Oriental was carrying his bow with an arrow nocked to the string.
Nor, despite being close to their destination, did they place
the weapons in less accessible positions. In fact, they grew
even more watchful.

Few people who knew Texas would have blamed the trio
for such behavior.

Even judged by the most tolerant standards, San Phillipe
was far from an attractive place. For a number of reasons,
particularly the presence of several dangerous reefs and
shoals offshore, it was not even a success as a port and served
mainly as a point at which small vessels could put in with

illicit cargoes. However, it had not been considered a suitable location for the *Bostonian Lady* to land the consignment of caplock rifles. There were ugly rumors that a number of the wrecks which had occurred in the vicinity might not have been accidental, but were caused through the ships being lured to destruction by the local inhabitants.

Although the time was close to midnight, most of the houses still had lamps burning and people moving about in them. Laughter, shouts, a rumble of conversation and music sounded from the largest building in the center of the town. However, while there did not appear to be anybody on the single street, the girl and the two young men were conscious of being watched.

"Blast it!" Di muttered, nodding toward the noisy and well illuminated building, but holding her voice down to little more than a whisper. "I was hoping that Cole Turtle'd be closed down afore we got here."

"The trouble with you is that you want everything too easy," Ole Devil replied, just as quietly and without relaxing his vigilance any more than the girl had while speaking. "What would this life of ours be without a little challenge or two and a few difficulties?"

"A damned sight easier," Di stated, *sotto voce.* "Which I'd sooner it son-of-bitching was, but don't reckon it's ever likely to get to be. And I don't want any old Nipponese sayings that *you've* just made up!"

"Humble self was not going to say a word," Tommy answered, the girl's last sentence having been addressed to him. "Let honorable and illustrious companions make foolish conversation while I keep watch over them."

"Why thank you 'most to death," Di sniffed, then went on as if to herself. "Damned if I know which of 'em's the worst. Ain't neither the one to improve on the other."

Glancing quickly at Di, Ole Devil found nothing to lessen

his admiration for the way in which she was bearing up under
what had been—and still was—a period of dire tribulation
and anxiety.

Doc Kimberley had done everything in his power, but Ewart Brindley's condition was still critical. Nor could moving
him have been achieved without much pain and the risk of
aggravating his injury still further. Yet there was a definite
limit to how long he could be allowed to stay where he was.
Not only was the weather far from ideal for a badly wounded
man to be out of doors, even though a shelter had been made
for him, the area he was in might—in fact, probably would—
be unsafe in the near future. Even accepting that Major
Abrahan Phillipe Gonzales *de* Villena *y* Danvila's deserted
mozo had spoken the truth, it would only be a matter of a few
days before the Arizona Hopi *Activos* Regiment put in an
appearance. There was also the possibility that Madeline de
Moreau might gather sufficient assistance, either from renegades or the Mexican Army, to make another bid at captur-
ing the assignment. So the old man would have to be taken
somewhere beyond their reach.

For all the great concern she was feeling over the welfare
of her grandfather and Joe Galton, who was her adoptive
brother and companion since they had been children, the girl
had neither said nor done anything that would have inter-
fered with the work in which she was involved. Instead, she
had accepted that both were receiving the best possible care
and had given her full attention to dealing with the urgent
problem of transporting the consignment.

With time of such vital importance, and there having been
nowhere else close by from which a mare might be obtained,
Ole Devil had set out for the town as soon as it was possible.
Being aware of the inhabitants' well-deserved unsavory reputation, he had realized that the visit would entail a considerable element of danger. He had doubted that, even though it

might be to their advantage to gain independence from the
rule of *Presidente* Antonio Lopez de Santa Anna, they would
allow thoughts of how useful the five hundred caplock rifles
would be in their fellow Texians' struggle against the numerical superiority of the Mexican Army to override their preda-
tory instincts. The weapons were too tempting a prize for
them to ignore and he had sufficient worries on his hands
already without creating more.

However, with Company "C" of the Texas Light Cavalry
already subdivided by the need to maintain a circle of pickets
around Santa Cristóbal Bay as well as guarding the consignment and the mule train, he was unable to bring a strong
enough force to ensure his safety. In fact, but for one detail,
he would have restricted his party to himself and the little
Oriental.

There was a man in San Phillipe, no more law abiding than
his neighbors, who owed Ewart Brindley a debt of gratitude
and could be counted upon to repay it. As he was, or had
been, a leader of the community, his support could spell the
difference between success and failure. However, being of a
suspicious nature, he would not have accepted either a verbal
or a written request from the wounded packmaster if it was
delivered by someone with whom he was not acquainted.
Galton was still too weakened by his injury to make the hard
and fast ride which the situation required. So Di, who Cole
Turtle knew and liked, had been given the task of enlisting
his aid.

In spite of their hopes that they might find an ally at San
Phillipe, the girl and her companions had made certain preparations which they believed would improve their chances of
survival.

Di had on a long and bulky wolfskin jacket and it did much
to conceal her well rounded feminine curves as well as the
pistol and knife on her waistbelt. By drawing down the wide

brim of her low-crowned, fawn-colored hat—which had been
hanging with the coat on her saddle when the *Bostonian
Lady*'s captain had studied her on his arrival at Santa Cristóbal Bay—she could partially hide her features and her hair
was short enough to attract no attention.

For his part, Ole Devil had retained his armament—with
the exception of the saber—which he had left in Mannen
Blaze's care—but exchanged his riding breeches for a pair of
yellowish-brown civilian Nankeen trousers from his war bag.

However, apart from donning a hat to be used for the
same purpose as the girl's head gear, lessening the chances of
his Oriental features being noticed, Tommy had not made
any alterations to his attire, weapons, or appearance.

As an added precaution, in case they should be seen arriving—which Di had claimed was practically inevitable—the
trio had made a wide detour around the town and were approaching it along the trail from the north. From what they
could see and hear, taken with the sensation of being
watched, they decided that the additional distance which
they had been compelled to cover so as to mislead such ob-
servers was worthwhile.

Drawing closer to the large building without being challenged or molested, Di and the two young men became
aware of a shape on the porch at the right of the open front
door. Conveying an impression of considerable size and bulk,
but wearing a high crowned black *sombrero* and a *serape*
which covered it from head to foot, the figure was squatting
with its back against the wall and appeared to be asleep.

"Could be's good ole Cole Turtle's still the head he-hooper
around these parts," the girl hissed, relief plain in her voice.
"That there's his man, Charlie Slow-Down, I told you
about. There's a full loaded and cocked blunderbuss under
his *serape,* which he's never been slow to use it. But do and
say like I told you and we'll be all right—I hope!"

"That's what I like," Ole Devil answered, studying the motionless shape. "A girl with confidence in her own advice."

"Ancient and wise Nipponese saying—" Tommy began.

"That's all we need!" Di groaned.

"Woman seldom speaks with wisdom," the little Oriental continued blandly. "And when she does, it is by accident."

"If things go wrong," the girl whispered, "I know who I hope gets shot first—and where he's hit."

For all their quietly spoken banter, Di, Ole Devil and Tommy appreciated that, far from being over, their problems could soon reach a crisis. The conversation was a way of reducing the tension which all of them were experiencing.

While confident that Cole Turtle would do what he could to help, Di had never minimized the risks involved by going to ask him for it. Strangers had never been made welcome in San Phillipe, unless they were sufficiently well armed and tough enough to make expressions of disapproval from the population inadvisable. What was more, almost two years had elapsed since her last visit. Turtle might have left during that time, or have lost his position of authority. Should either have happened, the trio might find it impossible to achieve their purpose. It could even prove difficult for them to escape with their lives.

Unfortunately, as the girl and her companions realized, the presence of Charlie Slow-Down in his usual position could not be regarded as conclusive evidence that the man whom they were hoping to contact was available. While the big Kaddo Indian had acted as Turtle's bodyguard, he could have transferred his loyalties to the new owner if the San Phillipe Hotel—by which grandiloquent name the establishment was known—had changed hands. However, they were aware that it was too late for them to turn back and attempt to satisfy their curiosity by some other, safer, means.

Neither increasing nor slowing their pace, although

Tommy returned the arrow to his quiver, the trio brought their mounts to a halt in front of the building and at the unoccupied half of the hitching rail. While doing so, they looked across at the half a dozen horses tethered on the other side. There was nothing significant about the various styles of saddles on the animals. It would be many years before the low horned, double girthed rig—designed for the specialized needs of the cattle industry as it would be practiced in the Lone Star State*—became almost *de rigueur* for Texians. Many colonists still used the outfits which they had brought with them, or sat Mexican saddles purchased locally.

On dismounting, Tommy hung the bow and quiver over his saddle horn. Effective as they would have been in the event of attempts to molest his party during the ride through the town, he preferred to rely upon his *daisho* of swords when on foot and at close quarters. However, Di and Ole Devil retained their rifles. Nor did they set the hammers at half cock before, having hung their reins over the hitching rail, they stepped on to the sidewalk.

"*Saludos,* Charlie Slow-Down," Ole Devil greeted, as he had been instructed by the girl, taking a buckskin pouch from the inside pocket of his shirt. "Ewart Brindley sent this snuff and said he'd be obliged if you'd keep an eye on our horses and gear while we're inside."

There was no verbal response to the request. However, a thick left wrist emerged from beneath the *serape.* Deciding that—with the possible exception of Mannen Blaze's hands —the upturned palm was the largest he had ever seen, Ole Devil dropped the pouch into it. Closing, the fist disappeared and the mound of humanity became as motionless as before.

---

* *The double girths were necessary because Texas cowhands scorned the use of a "dally," a half hitch which could be released immediately in an emergency, when roping. Instead, being determined to retain anything upon which they dropped a loop, they fastened the rope to the saddle horn.*

Satisfied that he had carried out and been accepted in a proscribed ritual, the Texian wished he had been given some indication of the state of affairs which was awaiting his party inside the hotel. Not that he gave any sign of his feelings. In fact, he had a gasconading swagger in his walk as, with the Browning rifle cradled on the crook of his left arm, he led the way across the porch. With the girl and the little Oriental following on either side and about a pace to the rear, he paused to let his eyes grow accustomed to the glare of the well-lit interior. Then he stepped through the double doors and his friends followed him.

The lateness of the hour did not appear to be having any adverse effect upon trade in the hotel's barroom. There were a number of men in various styles of clothing ranging from Eastern suits to buckskins and Mexican *charro* garments, but all had one thing in common. Every one was well armed, with pistols, knives, or both. A number of white, Latin and Indian girls in garish costumes circulated among the customers and helped to ensure that the two bartenders behind the counter —made from planks set on empty barrels—were kept occupied in dispensing their wares. Although the band, which was comprised of a piano, two fiddlers and a trumpeter, continued to play with no reduction of volume, conversations died away. Cold, hard, watchful eyes turned in the newcomers' direction.

Advancing to Ole Devil's right, with enough room for her to turn the rifle she was carrying into a firing position if the need arose, Di tried to walk in a cockily masculine fashion. She also scanned the room from beneath the drawn down brim of her hat, searching for the man who could mean the trio would achieve their purpose and be allowed to go without hindrance. Reaching a table in the right-hand rear corner, she was hard put to hold down an exclamation of relief.

There were many people in Texas and along the lower

reaches of the Mississippi River who would not have shared the girl's satisfaction over seeing the man who was responsible for it. In fact, they would have regarded such an emotion as peculiar when it was directed at Cole Turtle.

Even sitting down, Turtle was obviously tall and built on a massive scale. Completely bald, his fat and from a distance (but not when close enough to notice his hard eyes) jovial face sported an enormous black mustache. He wore an expensive gray cutaway coat, white shirt with a ruffed front and Nankeen trousers tucked into riding boots. Evidence of his prosperity was given by a couple of diamond rings and the pearl stickpin in his scarlet silk cravat. A good quality percussion-fired pistol lay close to his big right fist and there were four stacks of gold coins in front of him. Tossing down his cards, he let out a thunderous guffaw of laughter and scooped in the money which had formed the pot in the hand of poker which had just ended.

None of the other five players in the game appeared to find their heavily built host's actions amusing. Instead, they scowled at him and one angrily gathered the cards ready to continue. Ignoring his companions, Turtle glanced at the newcomers. After one quick look, he neither moved nor gave any indication of being aware that the trio had entered. For all that, he felt uneasy.

One of Charlie Slow-Down's functions was to prevent unauthorized visitors from coming in with such readily accessible weapons as the rifles carried by two of the new arrivals. Nor had he ever failed in the duty. Yet despite there being something which seemed vaguely familiar about the tall young man, Turtle could not remember having met him. Nor, due to the positions of their hats, could the hotelkeeper identify the other two.

Conscious of Turtle's scrutiny, brief as it had been, Di wished that she could inform her companions that this was the man they had come to meet. However, such was her faith in Ole Devil and Tommy, she felt sure that such an explanation would not be necessary. She had described Turtle for their benefit while riding to the town. Men of their ability could be counted upon to keep their eyes open and wits about them under such trying conditions. So they were sure to have already seen him and made a correct identification.

While the Texian and the little Oriental were justifying the girl's faith in their powers of observation, having noticed that Turtle was present, they were not devoting their entire attention to him. Instead, once they had seen and recognized him, they were studying the other occupants of the room.

Some of the furnishings of the barroom, particularly the counter, left much to be desired in style and elegance and made one fitting seem out of place. Taken from a wrecked vessel—which had gone aground on a local reef—having survived the impact and being brought ashore in a small boat, a large mirror was attached to the wall behind the bar. It was a fixture regarded with mixed feelings by the customers. However, as three men had already been killed because their behavior had been considered a menace to its existence and safety, it was now an accepted feature of the hotel.

While crossing the room, Ole Devil and Tommy were taking advantage of the mirror's most controversial and, to some of the clientele's way of thinking, objectionable qualities. Looking at the reflections on its surface, which was cleaned daily even though other parts of the establishment might not be, they were able to watch the people to their rear as well as keeping those in front and to either side under observation. They could tell that their arrival was a source of considerable interest and speculation, but that was only to have been expected. Strangers must be even rarer in San Phillipe since the struggle for independence had commenced than they had been in more peaceful times.

However, in spite of their curiosity, the majority of the customers had no intention of attempting to satisfy it. Many of them were residents of the town and most of the remainder had visited the hotel often enough to be aware of its most stringently enforced rule. Not only did the tall young man look as mean as hell and might prove dangerous if riled, but the fact that he and one of his companions carried rifles was significant. It suggested that they were sufficiently trusted by Cole Turtle to have the right to be armed in such a manner. Visitors who were less favored were compelled by Charlie Slow-Down to leave outside all but the weapons upon their persons.

Four men, who were occupying a table to the left of the door, struck Ole Devil as being more than casually interested in his party's arrival. Dressed in the kind of clothing which would evolve into the attire of the Texas cowhand, they were unshaven and travel-stained. Empty plates, a coffeepot and cups in front of them implied that they had not been present for long. In fact, even as the Texian gave the quartet his attention, a girl with a tray arrived and cleared the table.

Although Ole Devil could not recollect the circumstances, he was certain that he had come into contact with at least one of the quartet recently. However, he was unable to make a more extensive examination. Seated with his back to the trio, the man had been looking over his shoulder. Then, turning his head to the front, he began to speak to his companions.

Before the Texian could decide whether he was correct in his assumption, he saw certain disturbing movements by the rest of the quartet. The man nearest to the door and the one at the far side of the table dropped their hands out of his range of vision. However, the behavior of the last man supplied a clue to what they might be doing. He reached across with his right hand and grasped the butt of the pistol which

ALL YOURS FREE!

**ONE DOZEN BEAUTIFUL FOUR-COLOR
SCENES FROM THE OLD WEST IN THE**

LOUIS L'AMOUR
WALL CALENDAR

(An $8.99 value in stores)

SPECIAL · SPECIAL · SPECIAL

The best-selling novel:
SACKETT for only $4.95
in the hardbound Collector's Edition!

e Old West with
ompelling novel, *Sackett*,
ee!

l: You may keep *Sackett* for only $4.95!*

In Addition to the Free Louis L'Amour Calendar

. . . your risk-free preview volume of *Sackett* will introduce you to these outstanding qualities of the bookbinder's art—

- Each volume is bound in rich, rugged sierra-brown simulated leather.

- The bindings are sewn, not just glued, to last a lifetime. And the pages are printed on high-quality paper that is acid-free and will not yellow with age.

- The title and Louis L'Amour's signature are golden embossed on the spine and front cover of each volume.

SAVE OVER HALF OFF!

BUSINESS REPLY MAIL

FIRST CLASS MAIL   PERMIT NO. 2154   HICKSVILLE, NY

POSTAGE WILL BE PAID BY ADDRESSEE

The Louis L'Amour Collection
Bantam Doubleday Dell Direct, Inc.
PO Box 956
Hicksville NY 11802-9829

NO POSTAGE
NECESSARY
IF MAILED
IN THE
UNITED STATES

Detach and mail this postpaid card to get The Louis L'Amour Calenda absolute FREE!

was thrust through the left side of his belt. Before he could draw the weapon, an angry comment from the first to have attracted Ole Devil's attention caused him to refrain. If the way in which he glared at the mirror was any guide, he had been warned that his actions might have been seen via its reflection. He did not appear to be too pleased with what he was told next, but scowled and spoke heatedly.

After a brief discussion, the man with his back to Ole Devil shoved aside his chair and stood up. The rest also rose, with the second and third of them taking care to keep their right hands concealed behind their backs. Throwing another brief look across the room, the first man strode out of the door.

Suddenly, Ole Devil's memory clicked. Unless he was mistaken, the man had been a member of Madeline de Moreau's gang of renegades and had fled with her when Company "C" had put in its appearance to rout them.

Even as Ole Devil was reaching his conclusions regarding the identity of the man who was leaving the San Phillipe Hotel, he became aware of something else. Instead of following Dodd, as he remembered having heard their companion called, the other three from the table were walking toward the bar. They might merely be intending to buy drinks, but he doubted it.

In fact, the young Texian felt sure that two of the approaching men were holding cocked pistols concealed behind their backs!

If that was so, there could be only one reason for the three renegades' actions!

8

YOU *COULD* SAY THEY'RE ON OUR SIDE

"What do you make of it, Mister Blaze?" asked the sentry who was posted on top of the slope overlooking Santa Cristóbal Bay, at about the time that—some fifteen miles to the north—Ole Devil Hardin was identifying the member of Madeline de Moreau's band of renegades in the San Phillipe Hotel. Holding his voice down, he peered through the darkness in an attempt to see the approaching riders who, as yet, he could only hear. Failing to do so, he went on, "It can't be Cap'n Devil, Di 'n' Tommy. There's more 'n three of 'em and they're coming from the southwest."

"That's the living truth," Mannen Blaze conceded, sounding as if he was still more than half asleep. He had, however, been sufficiently awake to pick up and fit a five shot magazine into his Browning slide repeater rifle before leaving his blankets. "It's not them. You did right to call me."

"It might be some of your men from the mule train," Beauregard Rassendyll suggested, having been disturbed when the sentry had arrived to report to his superior that he had heard riders in the distance and had accompanied them to investigate.

"Only they ain't coming from the right direction for that, neither," the enlisted man pointed out, wondering somewhat irascibly why the dude—whom he had not bothered to waken—had come with them. "On top of which, they've been told to stay put 'n' guard the mules. And Cap'n Devil don't take kindly to folks going again' his orders."

"Who do you think it can be, Mannen?" Rassendyll inquired, far from pleased at the sentry's faintly derisive attitude; which had not been in evidence while the man was addressing the burly redhead.

"I wouldn't know and couldn't even start to guess," Mannen admitted, in tones redolent of disinterest. From the way in which he was speaking, his only desire was to get back to his blankets and interrupted sleep. "Whoever they are, they're not trying to sneak up on us."

"Could be they're just passing by, Mister Blaze," the sentry offered, far from being fooled by the other's air of lethargy. "We haven't got no fire, nor nothing else to show we're here."

"Could be," Mannen grunted, still with nothing to show he found the subject other than a boring interference with the more important business of resting. "I only hope's that's all there is to it."

"You haven't heard anything to suggest they've come across the pickets in that direction, have you?" Rassendyll asked, holding his Croodlom and Co. "Duck Foot" Mob Pistol in his right hand and wondering if he would find use for its special qualities.*

* The Croodlom & Co. "Duck Foot" Mob Pistol and similar weapons had four barrels fixed side by side and splayed out in the form of a fan, so that its bullets would spread when leaving the muzzles. They were popular with prison guards and the officers of merchant ships as a means of quelling an unruly crowd at close quarters.

"A thing like that's not real likely to slip my remembering, *mister*," the sentry answered indignantly.

"By the Lord!" Rassendyll began furiously, being accustomed to more respectful treatment from members of the lower social orders. "I've had ab—"

"Might be's well if we all talk softer," Mannen put in almost sleepily, but there was a hard timbre underlying his words.

"Sorry, Mister Blaze, sir," the sentry grunted, his attitude vastly different from when he had addressed the former supercargo of the *Bostonian Lady*. "What do *you* want for us to do?"

Rassendyll had been on the point of directing some of his wrath and indignation at the burly redhead, but common sense took control. Instead, he refrained from speaking and looked at the other with considerable interest. Up to that moment, he had always regarded Mannen as an amiable, exceptionally strong, yet—if not exactly slow-witted—dull and lazy young man who took little notice of what was going on around him.

Suddenly, Rassendyll realized that he had been comparing the burly redhead with Ole Devil and other more obviously competent members of the Hardin, Fog and Blaze clan. Since being left alone with Mannen, he had grown increasingly aware that he might have made an incorrect judgment. Certainly, none of the detail who were guarding the consignment had shown any concern over Ole Devil's departure, or hesitated to carry out Mannen's orders. The sentry's attitude was further evidence that there was more to the redhead than met the eye. Such respect had to be earned and was not given merely because the recipient had had the good fortune to be born into the right circles.

Having noticed the way Rassendyll had stiffened, then relaxed, but was still continuing to gaze at him in a speculative

fashion, Mannen guessed what had caused the behavior. He
was more amused than annoyed by the Louisianan's reaction. If it came to a point, he felt just a mite flattered. While
he had never imagined himself to be as brilliant as his cousin
Devil, he knew that he was competent enough to carry out
his duties without needing to have somebody hold his hand.
Yet it was satisfying when others, particularly a smart and
capable person like Rassendyll, also appreciated his good
qualities.

However, there were more important matters than self-
congratulation demanding Mannen's attention. As yet, the
approaching riders were still only noises which came ever
closer.

The questions which the burly Texian had to answer were,
who they might be and, more important, how to deal with
them.

Although Mannen did not reply to the sentry's request for
orders immediately, indecision was not keeping him silent.
Knowing the vitally important issues which were at stake, he
wanted to consider the matter before committing himself
and his men to any line of action.

Firstly, before any plans could be made, or orders given,
there was the matter of the riders' identity to be taken into
consideration.

The direction from which the party was coming suggested
that they might be members of the Arizona Hopi *Activos*
Regiment, but their apparent disregard for the need to travel
silently argued against such a solution. Suspecting that there
might be an enemy force in the vicinity, they would not be
likely to move through the darkness with so much noise. Unless, of course, they had learned of the consignment and its
location, so hoped their behavior would lull the guards into a
sense of false security.

Other Mexican soldiers could also be expected to come

from the southwest. If they had not made contact with the *Activos,* they might believe that there were no Texians around and therefore see no need to take precautions.

Or they could be renegades. Not Madeline de Moreau's band, who would know better than attempt such a subterfuge. There were other gangs, any of whom would be only too willing to make a stab at snatching off such valuable loot if they learned about it.

On the other hand, the riders could be members of the Republic of Texas's Army who had been sent to reinforce Company "C" and increase the chances of delivering the consignment safely. They could even be engaged upon some unconnected mission. Knowing how certain sections of the army were conducting themselves, Mannen felt that the arrival of a party who were on the latter kind of assignment might prove a mixed blessing and could even be a disadvantage.

Lastly, they could be no more than a bunch of ordinary civilians running away from the advancing Mexican Army. Such people were likely to make for the coast so as to join the northbound trail. Except that did not explain why they were traveling after nightfall. If the need to do so had been caused by the presence of a hostile force nearby, they should at least have been attempting to move in a quieter fashion.

The fact that there had been no warning from the pickets was not such a good sign as it might appear on the surface. There had not been sufficient men available to set out a ring of them through which it would be impossible for anybody to pass undetected. However, especially as the approaching party were not even trying to conceal their presence, they should have attracted at least one of the pairs of lookouts' attention. Once that had happened, following the orders they had been given, a man should have returned to announce that riders were coming. That such a message had not been received aroused disturbing possibilities. If a picket had fallen into hostile hands, they might have been tortured into betraying their companions. In which case, the men who were coming might act in such a way as to lessen the chances of their true purpose being suspected.

All in all, Mannen found himself faced with one hell of a difficult problem.

"Damn it all!" the burly redhead told himself, with a certain doleful satisfaction which he had found helpful as a means of reducing his tension in times of stress. "Whatever I do about them is bound to come out wrong."

However, there was no sign of indecision in the way that Mannen addressed his companions. From various slight sounds beyond the rim, he guessed that Sergeant Dale had also been aroused when the sentry came to tell him about the riders and was acting in a sensible fashion.

"Head back and fetch half of the men up here, Beau," Mannen ordered and, for all the lethargic way in which he was speaking, the words were a command rather than a request to a social equal. "Hold them just below the rim. Have Sergeant Dale keep the rest ready to fetch up the spare rifles if they're needed."

"Aye aye!" Rassendyll replied, giving the traditional seafarer's response to an order with an alacrity which he would not have shown five minutes earlier.

"Hey there!" yelled an unmistakably Anglo-Saxon voice, which had the tones of a poorly educated Southron's drawl in it. "This here's Sammy Cope 'n' I'm fetching in some fellers."

"That's young Sammy for sure," the sentry declared quietly. "And he don't sound like he's got a knife shoved again' his back to make him say it."

"It doesn't," Mannen conceded, although he also realized that—while competent to handle their duty—neither of the pickets to which the man in question belonged could be termed the most intelligent and discerning members of Company "C." They were, in fact, probably the two most likely to be duped by an enemy. So he went on, in what could only be described as a languid commanding hiss, "Challenge them!"

"You-all stay put a-whiles!" called the sentry, which might fall short of a formal "Halt, who goes there?" but proved adequate for the situation. "Who've you got with you, Sammy?"

"They're a bunch of fellers—" the original speaker commenced, still sounding unperturbed, as he and whoever was with him came to a halt while still beyond the trio on the rim's range of vision.

"I'm Major von Lowenbrau, with a patrol of the Red River Volunteer Dragoons!" interrupted a harder and more decisive voice, which—although speaking English fluently—held just a trace of a German accent. "We're coming to speak with your officers!"

"They're all right!" Rassendyll breathed, having guessed at the cause of the redhead's perturbation and sounding relieved.

"Sure," Mannen replied. "You *could* say they're on our side. Go fetch those fellers up here."

"But—" Rassendyll began, then remembered what the redhead had told him about one aspect of the current situation in Texas.

"Figure on them being a guard of honor to show our respect for such an important visitor," Mannen suggested, before the supercargo could comment upon the matter, his somnolent tones charged with grim urgency. "Only get them up here *pronto,* but quietly and have them keep out of sight below the rim."

"Very good!" Rassendyll assented and turned to hurry away.

"Damn it, man, what's wrong with you?" the Germanic voice of von Lowenbrau barked irritably. "Can we advance?"

"Tell them to come ahead real slow and easy," Mannen ordered *sotto voce*, as the man by his side looked to him for guidance. "And make them think I'm just helping you stand guard."

"Yo!" responded the sentry, showing no surprise at his superior's behavior.

One of the better informed members of Company "C," the enlisted man was aware of certain conditions which were prevailing. So he understood why Mannen was taking precautions which seemed more suitable for dealing with enemies than greeting men who were serving on the same side in the Texians' struggle for independence.

Among the many problems with which Major General Samuel Houston was having to contend was the way that a few senior officers in the Republic of Texas's Army were refusing to accept orders and abusing their positions of authority. Instead of conforming to the sound tactics he was advocating—which consisted of withdrawing to the east until the time, place and conditions were suitable for making a stand —two in particular were taking advantage of the lack of an effective disciplinary system and insisted upon conducting their own private campaigns.

Having declared that he had no intention of retreating and would hold the town of Goliad under his control, Colonel James W. Fannin was retaining his force of four hundred of the army's best-equipped soldiers who would have been infinitely more useful serving under Houston's direct command.*

Another of the dissidents, Colonel Frank Johnson, was making preparations for—as he grandiloquently put it—car-

* *The tragic consequences of Colonel James W. Fannin's decision are told in* GET URREA.

rying the war to the enemy by invading Mexico along the coast road. Using the prospect of the loot which was waiting to be collected, he was gathering supporters for the venture. Nor did he care from where they came, or how they might affect the overall campaign. In fact, Ole Devil and Mannen had been responsible for the disruption of an attempt by one of his officers to persuade members of the regiments loyal to Houston that they would be better off in his service.

The Red River Volunteer Dragoons were a regiment— although, like most of the others in the Republic of Texas's newly formed and privately recruited army, its strength was not much over one hundred and fifty officers and men—who were prominent as adherents to Johnson's force. So the sentry could appreciate his superior's disinclination to trust its members.

"Come ahead, gents," the enlisted man requested. "Only do it real slow 'n' easy. We've had trouble with renegades and aim to make sure of who you are before you get too close."

"Good thinking!" Mannen praised, knowing that such a precaution would be understandable when taken for the reason which had been given.

"I hope Sammy's got enough sense not to give you away when he sees you're with me," the sentry replied. "I wouldn't think him and his amigo know how things stand 'tween General Sam and Johnson, so they've probably already told that major about the rifles."

That was a point which Mannen had also anticipated. While loyal enough, Cope and the man who was with him had never struck the redhead as being the kind to take an interest in something as remote as their superiors' policies beyond how they would be involved personally. Having no wish to emphasized the dissension among the senior officers, Ole Devil had advised Mannen and his non-coms to avoid referring to Johnson's plans. Some of the shrewder of the other ranks might have heard of it, but he doubted whether that would apply to the pair in question. So, seeing no harm in it and proud that their Company had been selected to handle such an important assignment, they would not be likely to speak other than the truth if asked by von Lowenbrau—as they were certain to have been—why they were on picket duty so far from the area in which the Texas Light Cavalry should be serving.

"Damn it, man!" bellowed the Dragoon major, but without setting his horse into motion. "I've told you who I am!"

"So did them renegades, 'cepting *they* wasn't who they claimed and I'm not about to take no chances," the sentry answered, once again supplying an understandable explanation for his behavior and went on to give a further demonstration of his intelligence. "I'd be a heap happier happen I knowed you'd let Sammy go back to his *amigo* on picket duty."

"Aw hell, Smithie—" Cope began, identifying the sentry's voice and seeing his chance of rejoining his companions by the bay.

"Get going!" von Lowenbrau interrupted, with anything but good grace.

"But—" Cope commenced.

"Do as you're told, blast you!" the major thundered, furious that his plans were suffering such a disruption.

"Call out when you're well on your way, Sammy-boy!" the sentry advised.

"You'll have rank as corporal comes Cousin Devil getting back," Mannen promised, nodding his approval.

"Gracias," the enlisted man replied and, as they heard a horse moving away, he went on, "I hope he doesn't yell too soon. Once he has, I can't keep on stalling them."

Looking over his shoulder, Mannen blessed his good fortune in having subordinates who were capable of intelligent thought. Clearly Sergeant Dale appreciated the situation without the need for lengthy explanations. He was personally leading the men up the slope and they were holding the noise of their ascent to the minimum.

From the bottom of the slope came a sudden, tiny red glow accompanied by a shower of minute sparks and barely audible—at that distance—popping sounds. A low curse burst from Mannen and he wondered what Rassendyll, the most likely culprit, was doing. Clearly he had lit one of those new-fangled friction matches* which were starting to replace the "Instantaneous Light Box"† and similar devices as a means of producing a fire. The matches were as yet not readily available in Texas, but could be obtained in the more civilized parts of the United States.

"Seems like Sammy's smarter'n we figured, Mister Blaze," remarked the sentry, whose name was Smith even before he had arrived in Texas, bringing the redhead's attention from the bottom of the valley. "He's not yelled and those fellers aren't moving in yet either."

By the time Cope declared that he had taken his departure without hindrance and, somewhat sarcastically, von Lowenbrau had requested permission to approach, Sergeant Dale had brought his men to positions just below the rim. Whatever had caused Rassendyll to strike a match still was not apparent to Mannen, but he could see the supercargo coming from the bottom of the valley at a swift but quiet run.

However, the redhead had things other than the super-

---

* The first practicable friction matches were marketed in 1827 by, among others, John Walker of Stockton-on-Tees, England, who called his product the "100 Sulphurata Hyperoxegenta Frict" match.
† "Instantaneous Light Box": consisting of a bottle containing sulphuric acid which was used to ignite wooden slivers—known as "splints"—tipped with a potassium chlorate, sugar and gum arabic compound. In the United States of America, a box with fifty "splints" retailed for two dollars, or four cents a light.

cargo's behavior to demand his attention. In a few seconds, as they began to come into sight, he was able to confirm what he had already suspected. Major von Lowenbrau's party was around thirty strong. While there were fifty non-coms and men in Company "C," half had been assigned to protect the halted mule train and were too far away to hear shooting at the bay. Putting out the seven two-man pickets had been a sensible precaution, but it had seriously depleted the numbers of the guard on the consignment. Even though Dale had exceeded the half which he had been ordered to bring, that still only put eight men—including Dale, but not counting Rassendyll and Mannen—on the upper reaches of the slope. However, every one was carrying three loaded caplock rifles as well as his personal weapons.

"Hold it there until you're identified 'n' Cap'n Hardin says you can come on!" Smith ordered, without the need for prompting, when the foremost of the riders was about thirty feet away, and he emphasized his words by cocking his rifle.

"Halt—!" snorted von Lowenbrau, although his military training secretly approved of the precaution and he wished that the men under his command would display an equal efficiency when carrying out their duties.

"Come on up here, you fellers!" called Mannen, adopting a coarse tone more suitable to an enlisted man than an officer, when the command did not meet with instant obedience. "They ain't doing it!"

Immediately, Dale's detail advanced into view and the redhead discovered why Rassendyll had struck the match. What was more, he heartily approved of what he had previously regarded as an inexplicable and possibly ill-advised action.

A beam of light stabbed from the bull's-eye lantern, which had been part of the supercargo's luggage along with the Mob Pistol that he was still holding, as his left hand shook open its front shield. While it did not have the brilliance of

later electric battery powered flashlights, it was still sufficient
to illuminate the man who was leading the newcomers and, if
his annoyed reaction proved anything, it at least partly dazzled him.

Tall, well built, sitting a fine-looking horse with a stiff-
backed military carriage, Major Ludwig won Lowenbrau
wore clothes more suitable to a professional gambler from a
Mississippi riverboat than a former officer—if of two grades
lower rank than he now laid claim to—in the Prussian Army.
However, his close-cropped blond hair, mustache drawn to
spikes and held there by wax, and the dueling scars on his
cheeks were indications of his background to those who
knew the signs.

No matter why he had "gone to Texas," von Lowenbrau—
who had once borne an even more distinguished name pre-
ceded by the honorific *"Freiherr,"* Baron—was far from being
a reckless fool. Sent by his colonel, for whom he had little
respect as an officer or a man, to take possession of the
consignment of caplock rifles which a spy on Houston's staff
had reported would be arriving at Santa Cristóbal Bay, he
was aware of what he would be up against. Even without the
support of Ewart Brindley's Tejas Indian mule packers, who
had a reputation for salty toughness and the ability to protect
any property under their care, Company "C" of the Texas
Light Cavalry outnumbered the small force which had grudg-
ingly been given to him.

Having met Ole Devil Hardin in the early days of the conflict, von Lowenbrau regarded him as being a potentially capable and efficient officer. Nor had anything he had seen so
far caused him to revise the opinion. Traveling through the
darkness in the hope of reaching his destination and moving
in shortly before the escort woke up in the morning, he had
been intercepted by the picket. Although he had satisfied its
members that he was an ally, neither had told him of their

exact reason for being so far away from their regiment. They had been equally uncommunicative about the other details which he had hoped to learn. Clearly they had been ordered to keep their mission a secret, even from other members of the Republic of Texas's Army, and they had insisted that their officers would answer all the questions. He had been too wise to force the issue. Nor had he been able to dissuade Cope from accompanying his party, to "show them the best way." The soldier's presence had ruined any chance of taking the rest of the escort unawares. From what he could see, they were alert and ready to take any action which might be necessary.

"Whose command is this?" the major asked, halting his horse and signaling for his men to stop as he realized that the light from the lantern would make him an easy target.

"Captain Hardin's Company 'C,' Texas Light Cavalry," Mannen replied, although he suspected that the information was unnecessary. "He's taken a detail to change the pickets."

"Can we make camp with you for the night?" von Lowenbrau inquired.

"If you're so minded," Mannen answered. "But we've got six men down there with what could be yellow fever, so we'd be obliged if you'd stand watch up here for us."

"Yellow fever!" several voices repeated from the major's rear, showing alarm.

"Quiet!" von Lowenbrau roared, checking the undisciplined chatter instinctively, but he knew the damage was done. Fear of the dreaded disease would make his men reluctant to enter the hollow. "Are you sure of it?"

"We've a man who knows enough about medical matters to know it when he sees it," Mannen declared, which was true as far as it went. "So you could help us plenty if you'd stand guard up here. We drove those renegades off, but they might be back."

For a moment, von Lowenbrau stood in silence. Having made Mannen's acquaintance also, he had formed a less favorable impression than that which Ole Devil had made upon him. So he did not believe that the redhead would have sufficient intelligence to make up such a story, nor to command that kind of disciplined obedience from the men of their company. What was more, the sentry had implied that Hardin was close at hand.

Another thought came to the major. A man as shrewd as young Hardin would know of Johnson's activities and about the Red River Volunteer Dragoons' support for them. So he would be wary of its members. In which case, he might have made up the story about the yellow fever to keep von Lowenbrau's party away from the consignment. Trying to ignore the request to stand guard could be very dangerous in that case.

"Of course we'll do as you ask, Mister Blaze," the major declared.

Although Mannen had hoped to bring about such a result, he knew that the trouble was far from over. Once the sun came up, von Lowenbrau would know how few men he had at his disposal to protect the consignment.

9

I WANT HIM ALIVE AND TALKING

Clearly Madeline de Moreau had been even more intelligent in her planning than Ole Devil Hardin had imagined. Not only had she selected a way to delay the mule train while she gained additional reinforcements to capture it, she had anticipated how he would react to the situation. Guessing that he would try to obtain a replacement for the dead bell mare from the nearest source, she must have sent some of her men to intercept whoever came. Possibly, being aware of the town's unsavory reputation, she had even deduced that he would take the risks involved by coming himself. If so, hating him for having killed her husband, she could have made arrangements to ensure her vengeance.

Having drawn his conclusions, Ole Devil diverted his full attention to solving the problems which he envisaged would arise from them. Much as he would have liked to do so, there was no safe way in which he could warn Diamond-Hitch Brindley and Tommy Okasi of the latest developments. Nor, with the brims of their hats drawn down to hide their features, could he tell if they realized the danger. To have spoken, as might have seemed the most obvious way, would have

informed the three men that their purpose had been suspected and might have made them launch their attack immediately instead of waiting until they were nearer. The trouble
with that was they were still well beyond the distance where
the little Oriental could hope to protect himself with his
swords. So, in addition to lulling them into a sense of false
security, allowing them to come closer would increase
Tommy's chances of survival. It would also make dealing with
them much easier—but only if the Texian's companions were
alerted to the situation.

Taking one factor into consideration as he watched the
three men without allowing his scrutiny to become obvious,
Ole Devil decided that he could delay warning his companions for a little while longer. The renegade who had been
prevented from drawing his pistol was following the girl.
From what he knew of her, the Texian was confident that she
was capable of taking care of herself for at least sufficient
length of time to let him render his assailant *hors-de-combat*
and go to her aid.

Apparently the trio did not intend to take any action until
the empty-handed man was within reaching distance of his
victim. Ole Devil decided that must have been what the final,
brief, discussion with Dodd was about. Having been denied
an opportunity to draw his pistol, the renegade would not
want the attack to be launched before he was close enough to
avoid being shot. No matter why they had elected to deal
with the situation in such a manner, the Texian felt that it was
improving his friends' chances of survival.

Provided, of course, that Di and Tommy were aware of
what was happening!

Ole Devil wished that he could tell whether they were or
not.

However, the Texian realized that the question would very
soon be answered.

Having advanced at a faster pace than their intended victims, the renegades were only about three paces behind the girl and the little Oriental. Although a number of the customers were able to see the pistols held by the center and left-hand men, it was typical of the type of people who came to San Phillipe that nobody gave a warning. For all that, the interest which some of the crowd were displaying served to notify the Texian that something was amiss, even if he had not already been aware of it.

In one respect, the attitudes of the onlookers raised another problem for Ole Devil. Were any of them in cahoots with the renegades?

The Texian was inclined to think that they were not. As Dodds's party had been alone at the table and, apparently, had only been there for a short time, they might have come in for a meal. In all probability, they had not expected him and his companions to arrive and were merely trying to take advantage of the situation.

At which point, Ole Devil was compelled to turn his attention from such speculations. As there was still nothing to inform him of Di's and Tommy's state of readiness, he tensed and prepared to warn them. Even as he was reaching the decision, the little Oriental's right hand rose as if to thrust back his hat.

Before Ole Devil could speak, Tommy demonstrated that he—for one—appreciated the situation and had made plans to deal with it. Raising his right hand had been a ploy to distract attention from his other actions. Closing his left fingers and thumb around the hilt of the *tachi*, he pulled forward and up until the blade was clear of the scabbard. At the same time, instead of continuing to walk forward, he stepped to the rear.

"Kiai!" the little Oriental yelled, bringing down his left arm with the same rapidity that it had risen.

Driving his left hand rearward, with the *tachi*'s blade extending below its heel instead of ahead of the thumb and forefinger, Tommy sent the inverted "beak" point into his would be assailant's solar plexus. The speed with which the little Oriental had drawn the sword and the unconventional manner in which he was wielding it, aided by his unexpected change of direction, gave the renegade no chance to take evasive action. Nor, although the man had just started to bring the pistol from behind his back, was he able to use it and save himself. Pain numbed him and, as he stiffened involuntarily, the weapon slipped from his fingers.

Like his companion, the second pistol-toting renegade was commencing to bring the firearm into use. While he was clearly startled by the discovery that at least one of their proposed victims had guessed what they were planning to do, he refused to become flustered. In fact, the urgency created by the changed conditions gave an added speed to his movements. Without giving a thought to avenging his stricken fellow conspirator, he devoted all his energies to the task to which he had been assigned, killing the young Texian.

When Dodd had refused to let the third man draw his pistol, he had insisted that he should be allowed to tackle the least dangerous member of the trio. Agreeing, Dodd had ordered that the girl must be taken alive. She would make a useful hostage and, even if her grandfather was dead, the Texians might turn over the consignment as the price for her liberation.

With that in mind, the renegade had decided how he would capture Di. Six foot tall and muscular, he had size, weight, strength and the element of surprise in his favor. So he meant to step up and enfold her in his arms from behind. Wanting to avoid a premature attack, he had allowed his companions to draw slightly ahead. Doing so had allowed him to watch for a signal from them and had also enabled him to keep the girl under observation.

Seeing the other two's pistols beginning to move forward, the man knew that the moment for action had come. So he lunged in the apparently unsuspecting girl's direction and his big hands reached out to grab her. He was already in motion before he realized that things were not going exactly as he had anticipated.

Despite having hoped for such a result, Ole Devil was surprised by the way in which the little Oriental was handling the situation. The left-handed draw was a trick that he had never seen before. Not that he gave the matter any thought. There was something of far greater importance demanding his complete attention.

In the interests of preventing the renegades from realizing that he had recognized them for what they were, Ole Devil had allowed his right hand to dangle at his side. It flashed on to the Browning rifle's stock as he swiveled from the hips to his left. Although the hand took hold and its forefinger entered the trigger guard, he made no attempt to lift the weapon from the crook of his left elbow. With the man's pistol swinging in his direction, he knew there would not be time for him to do so.

Unlike Ole Devil and Tommy, Di had not noticed the renegades. Instead, she had been watching the customers ahead and to her right. As these had not been able to see the pistols in the renegades' hands, they were doing nothing to alert her of the danger. Hearing Tommy's spiritual cry, which she identified for what it was, caused her to lift her head. It was her intention to look around and find what, or whom, the little Oriental was attacking. Instead, as her gaze reached the reflection in the bar's mirror, she discovered that there was a big man approaching, clearly intending to catch hold of her.

The sight came as one hell of a shock to the girl!

The Texian realized that the little Oriental had his part in the affair under control, which did not come as any surprise. However, he was equally aware that the danger was still far from ended. Nor, much as he would have liked, could he devote any attention to how the girl was faring. The renegade to his rear had to be stopped—and fast!

Swiveling to the left at the hips, Ole Devil pointed the Browning by instinctive alignment. At such close range, he felt that it would be sufficiently accurate for his needs and, of infinitely greater importance under the circumstances, faster than any other method. With the barrel directed in what he believed to be the required area, his forefinger squeezed the trigger. If he missed, there would not be time for him to carry out the simple manipulation of his rifle's mechanism which would allow him to fire again.

With the blade of his *tachi* sinking into its recipient's flesh like a hot knife passing through butter, Tommy flashed a glance to discover how his companions—the girl in particular —were faring. He realized that, due to the attacks having been launched almost simultaneously, she would have to fend for herself until either he or Ole Devil was able to go to her aid. Twisting and starting to step to the right so as to avoid the stricken renegade and draw free his weapon, he watched the third man rushing toward Di and realized that she had not equaled his speed in becoming aware of the danger.

Even as Tommy came to his disturbing conclusion, Di looked up. Conditioned by her way of life to react swiftly and sensibly in the face of danger, she displayed remarkable presence of mind. Accepting that there would not be time to turn and defend herself with the rifle, she made no attempt to do so. Nor did she try to avoid her assailant by leaping forward or aside. With his hands almost upon her, she dropped into a crouching posture with her right knee on the floor.

Much to his mortification, the burly renegade found that his objective was disappearing from his range of vision just as he was confident that he had her at his mercy. Carried onward by his momentum, he tripped over her and, turning a half somersault, alighted supine and with a bone-jolting impact.

Up flicked the hammer of Ole Devil's rifle, setting off the chain reaction which it was designed to create. There was a crack and flame gushed from the muzzle, followed by a swirling mass of white powder smoke. Before the renegade's pistol could point at the Texian, a conical .45-caliber bullet slammed into the center of his chest. There was an audible crack as it broke the breast bone and passed through to reach the vital organs of the torso. Slipping from its owner's hand, the pistol landed on the floor and fired, but its ball flew harmlessly to hit one of the barrels which were supporting the counter.

Although the man's collision with Di had not been gentle, she had braced herself in anticipation of it. So, despite having her hat knocked off, she was able to retain her equilibrium. Straightening up almost as soon as her assailant struck the floor, she threw a quick look which assured her that there was no cause for alarm so far as her companions were concerned. Smoke was still curling out of the barrel of Ole Devil's Browning and his right thumb was operating the lever on the side of the frame so as to cause the next chamber of the magazine to move into alignment with the bore. Twirling around, the man he had shot was going down. Beyond them, Tommy had withdrawn his *tachi* and, clutching at the wound, the stricken renegade was collapsing to his knees with his face showing horror and agony.

Startled expressions were bursting from all sides. Chairs rasped, or were thrown over, as their occupants began to rise hurriedly. Every nonparticipating person in the barroom stared at the group which was the center of attraction. The fact that one of the involved parties had proved to be a good-looking girl, who showed herself to be as capable as either of her companions, gave added spice to the drama.

Cole Turtle had been an interested onlooker from his place at the big stake poker game over which he was presiding. While he had noticed that one of the men who was following the newcomers carried a concealed pistol, he had not offered to intervene. He was puzzled by how the trio, none of whom he had been able to identify, managed to pass Charlie Slow-Down with two of their number carrying rifles. However, he had felt that it was not his place to intrude upon what was clearly a private matter. His curiosity could be satisfied after the affair had run its course.

"Well I'm damned!" Turtle spat out, his eyes focusing on the girl.

Before the hotelkeeper could say or do anything more, there was an interruption.

When Dodd had sent his companions to deal with Ole Devil's party, using the valid excuse that he might be remembered from the previous day's fighting, whereas they had not arrived until long after it was over, he had promised to support them from outside if necessary. Leaving the building, he had done no more than glance at and dismiss as of no importance the motionless and, apparently, fast asleep Kaddo Indian. Instead, he had drawn and cocked his pistol. Then he waited to see if he would be required to take a hand.

Watching what was happening, the renegade felt no remorse over his companions' failure and fate. His whole attention was being devoted to considerating what would be the most advisable line of action, concluding that discretion was of far greater value than valor under the circumstances. According to Madeline de Moreau, Ole Devil Hardin's rifle could be fired a number of times without needing to be recharged in the normal manner. Even if she had misunderstood its qualities, or was exaggerating for some reason, the girl held what was almost certain to be a loaded rifle. So, to Dodd's way of thinking, the most sensible thing to do was withdraw.

On the point of departing, Dodd saw an objection to doing so until he had taken care of another matter. While two of his companions were either dead or close to it, the third had survived. He had toppled over the girl's back when she had ducked to avoid his hands, but was already trying to sit up and did not appear to be too seriously injured.

For a moment, Dodd thought that the problem would be solved without the need for any action on his part. Seeing the man was still capable of movement, the girl took the rifle from across her left arm. Grasping it in both hands, she raised it ready to drive its butt against his head. Such an attack could easily prove fatal, particularly when it was being delivered in the heat of anger by somebody as quick tempered as Di Brindley.

Unfortunately for Dodd, Ole Devil was equally aware of the possibility.

"Hold it, Di!" the Texian snapped. "I want him alive and talking!"

Hearing his employer's words, Tommy Okasi transferred the *tachi* to his right hand and bounded forward. He angled the blade so that its point, coated with the blood of the man he had stabbed, was in an ideal position to be driven into the renegade's chest.

"D—Don't!" the man yelped, staring at the *tachi* with horror and making no further attempt to rise. "I—I quit!"

Although the renegade did not know it, he was in far greater danger from the girl whom he had tried to attack than the grim-faced "Chinaman" as he assumed Tommy to

be. There were *very* few people who could have prevented
her from smashing the butt of the rifle on his head by speaking. However, such was the respect in which she now held
Ole Devil that she was willing to yield to his demand.

"Aw shucks, Devil!" Di protested, lowering the weapon.
"You don't let a gal have any fun at a—"

A commotion just outside the building brought the girl's
words to an end.

Realizing that the Mephistophelian-featured Texian intended to take a living and, given suitable inducements, information supplying prisoner, Dodd knew what must be
done. So he lifted his pistol to shoulder level and with both
hands. He was about to take aim into the room when there
was a movement to his left. Glancing in that direction, he
received a shock.

Either the man who was squatting by the entrance had
woken up, or—which seemed more likely—he had not been
asleep!

A savage face showed from below the brim of the *sombrero,* but that was not the main cause of alarm for Dodd.
Looking as large as a cannon under the circumstances, the
bell mouth of a blunderbuss was pointing in his direction
from beneath the *serape.*

Even as the renegade was taking in the sight, there was a
puff of white smoke from the priming pan of the Indian's
weapon. Then, with a thunderous roar, it vomited a spray of
buckshot balls which encompassed him and ripped his torso
into gory doll rags. Thrust sideways by their impact, he
twirled and measured his length facedown on the sidewalk.

As always, Charlie Slow-Down had done his duty. Noticing
Dodd's furtive behavior on leaving the building, he had been
alert for the possibility of trouble. On hearing the crack of
Ole Devil's rifle, he had drawn the correct conclusion as to

who was involved. He also remembered that the newcomers had given the name of one of his employer's friends. So he had prevented the renegade from taking any part in the affair.

10
HOW MANY OF YOU WANT TO DIE?

Despite the urgency of dealing with his assailant, Ole Devil Hardin had not forgotten that Dodd was somewhere outside the San Phillipe Hotel. Even as the man he had shot was going down, he had seen the renegade standing on the sidewalk. However, before he could take any more positive action than completing his turn instead of remaining swiveled at the hips, Charlie Slow-Down's blunderbuss had removed any need for him to do so.

Satisfied that Dodd no longer posed a problem, the Texian swung his gaze around the barroom. The majority of the customers were on their feet and, although as yet none of them were making out-and-out threatening gestures, most were reaching for weapons. So he could not be sure of what their sentiments might be over the interruption to their pleasure.

Alert for the possibility that there were other renegades, or people in sympathy with them, present, Ole Devil kept his Browning Slide Repeating rifle in a position of readiness. He did not worry about the surviving member of the quartet who had tried to attack his party, being confident that Tommy

Okasi could keep the man under control. Knowing the kind of customer Cole Turtle's establishment attracted, he wished they had not discovered that Diamond-Hitch Brindley was a girl.

For her part, although just as appreciative of the situation, Di was much less perturbed than the Texian. In fact, she believed that the loss of her hat and exposure of her features had reduced rather than added to the danger. Provided, of course, that Turtle recognized her.

"Why howdy there, Di," the hotelkeeper boomed, his voice that of a well-educated Southron, rising with considerable alacrity despite his bulk. "It's good to see you again. Is your grandfather with you?"

Carrying around the room, Turtle's words were as much an announcement as a greeting, Ole Devil decided as he watched the effect they were having. They were stating that he not only knew the girl, but was showing his support for her and her companions. Taking notice, the customers realized that it would be unwise—to say the least—to become involved. Not that any of them had cause to do so. As far as they were concerned, the affair had been between two parties of strangers and was none of their concern.

"Sorry about causing the fuss, Cole, although it wasn't our fault's it happened," the girl replied, returning the rifle to the crook of her left elbow after setting its hammer at half cock. As Ole Devil duplicated the actions and Tommy wiped the blade of his *tachi* on his victim's shirt, she went on, "You saw the way it was, they didn't leave us any other choice."

"They didn't," Turtle conceded, sitting down again. "Are there likely to be any more of them looking for you?"

"Couldn't rightly say offhand," Di admitted and made a contemptuous gesture with her right thumb at the seated and frightened-looking renegade. "Maybe this yahoo'd like to tell us. What do you reckon, Devil?"

"I reckon he might feel obliging," the Texian replied, wishing that the girl had been more careful in the selection of her words. However, although the crowd were listening, nobody appeared to have noticed the clue to his identity which she had given. Scowling at the man, his voice hardened as he continued, "On your feet and shed your weapons, *hombre. Pronto!*"

Aided by a threatening gesture from Tommy's *tachi*, which looked no less deadly despite having had the blood cleaned from its blade, the order was obeyed with promptitude. Hurriedly scrambling up, the man discarded his pistol and knife in a manner which left no doubt that he did not intend to use either as a means of resisting his captors. Returning the sword almost as swiftly as it had been drawn, the little Oriental gathered up the weapons.

"Yes sir." Di grinned, noticing how the renegade was staring with awestricken fascination at the smaller of her male companions. Clearly the man had been impressed by the demonstration of *lai jitsu* in reverse and realized that, swiftly as the *tachi* had been returned to its sheath, it could be produced with an equal or possibly even greater speed. "He just might at that."

"Bring him over so that he can answer Mister Turtle's question, Tommy," Ole Devil commanded.

Having delivered his instructions, the Texian turned around. His whole bearing was redolent of confidence that he would be obeyed. Not only did the girl share his conviction that the little Oriental could handle their prisoner, but she knew why Ole Devil was acting in such a manner. He meant to impress the onlookers and warn them that he was a man with whom it would be dangerous to meddle. So she accompanied him as he strode across the room.

Approaching their host's table, Di gave the other men at it more of her attention than she was devoting to Turtle. All had an air of prosperity, but that was only to be expected. A player needed to have plenty of money, or negotiatable property, to sit in on a game with the kind of stakes for which they had been playing. Three were prominent members of the community, with only slightly lower social standing than the hotelkeeper, whom she knew slightly and did not care for. Nor did the other two, one in the attire of a civilian ship's officer and the other dressed in the fashion of a Mississippi riverboat gambler, strike her as being any more likable. She noticed that the latter was studying Ole Devil with considerable interest.

"Go after Devil-San!" ordered the little Oriental, picking up the pistol and knife without taking his eyes off the renegade.

Gulping nervously, despite having an even greater size and weight advantage than he had had over the girl, the man showed no inclination to refuse. Instead, he turned to scuttle after Di and Ole Devil. Tucking the pistol into his belt, Tommy followed at a more leisurely pace.

"All right, *hombre,*" the Texian said, his face taking on its most Satanic expression as the man came up. "You heard Mister Turtle. How many more of your outfit are there and how close might they be?"

"I—" the prisoner began, torn between fear of his captors and the knowledge of the way a betrayal would be regarded by his fellow renegades no matter how it had been extracted from him. "Augh!"

The last exclamation had been involuntary and was one of agony. It was caused by Tommy driving his right hand, with the fingers extended and the thumb bent across the palm, in a *hira-nukite*—four finger piercing—thrust against the man's kidney region. It was a most painful form of treatment, as its recipient might have testified if he had not had more urgent matters on his mind.

"You'll find it's a whole heap easier on yourself if you answer," Ole Devil remarked. "That was only for starters."

"There's a dozen more of us," the renegade croaked, having reached a similar conclusion. "The—They're about three miles out, on the trail south."

"Are they likely to come here?" Ole Devil asked.

"N—No!" the man yelped. "Honest to Gawd! Mrs. de Moreau allowed that you'd be sure to come that way and didn't even want us four to come in. How the hell did they miss—"

"We're asking the questions," Ole Devil pointed out.

"N—No offense!" the prisoner squawked, drawing in his spine as he anticipated the arrival of another painful blow from what had felt like a blunt steel spike.

"What're you laying for these folks over?" asked the gambler, who had been sharing his attention between the girl and the Texian.

"With respect, sir," Ole Devil put in before the renegade could answer, having no wish for the other occupants of the barroom to learn about the consignment of caplock rifles. "But that's between *them* and *us.*"

"Is that so?" The gambler growled, for the way in which the statement had been made was less polite than the words themselves.

"That's how *I* see it!" Ole Devil declared, his voice and attitude showing he considered the matter to be closed.

"Well I don'—" the gambler began.

"I'm not acquainted with either of these gentlemen, *Mister* Trellis," Cole Turtle interrupted, laying his big right hand on the butt of the pistol in what some people might have regarded as a casual, or even accidental, manner. "But Di Brindley and her grandfather are my friends."

"It seems I've the advantage over you in one respect," Wade Trellis replied, without making any great effort to hide his resentment over the hotelkeeper's intervention. He indicated the young Texian. "He's Ole Devil Hardin—"

"I'd an idea that he might be," Turtle admitted with a sardonic smile. "You're traveling in distinguished and influential company, Di."

"There's some's'd say better your'n, Cole," the girl answered, darting a hostile glare at the gambler.

"And what the nut-man* here's going to say next, sir," Ole Devil went on, "is that there used to be a price on my head in Louisiana."

"Used to be?" Trellis repeated, his cheeks reddening although he tried to keep from showing his resentment at having been classified as a "nut-man."

"Used to be," Ole Devil confirmed. "I've been told that my name's been cleared and the charge which brought me here no longer applies."

"So that's what you've heard, huh?" Trellis sneered.

"Di's here as your guest and under your protection, sir," Ole Devil said, ignoring the gambler and addressing the hotelkeeper in tones intended to carry around the room. He was aided by the silence which had descended upon the employees and customers alike. "But I can protect myself."

"That's understood, Captain Hardin," Turtle replied, speaking just as loudly and, as was obvious to everybody present, once again giving what amounted to his seal of approval for the Texian.

"Take this, Tommy," Ole Devil ordered, handing his rifle to the little Oriental. Then he swung his cold, Satanic gaze to Trellis. "The news was brought by a friend, whose word I

* Nut-man: operator of a "shell game," using a dried pea and three walnut shells or thimbles, such as is described in THE LAW OF THE GUN. As the game is purely a swindle, despite requiring considerable manipulative skill, a nut-man was not regarded very highly in gambling circles.

trust, so *I* believe it, *nut-man.* If *you'd* care to dispute the story, pick up Mister Turtle's pistol and start to do it."

Looking from the grim-faced young Texian to the gambler and back, a broad grin twisted the hotelkeeper's lips. After a glance at Di, who neither moved nor spoke, he set the hammer of the pistol at half cock and pushed across the table until it was just within the gambler's reach. Then, taking his hand away, he sat back with an air of eager anticipation. His whole attitude showed that he expected, hoped even, that the challenge would be accepted. Knowing Trellis, he did not doubt it would.

Nor was Turtle particularly surprised that Ole Devil should be adopting such a high handed attitude. It was typical of an arrogant, hot tempered young Southron blood that he would be quick to respond to any suggestion which might affect his honor. Or even merely because he had, for some reason, taken a dislike to another person.

For all the apparently impassive way in which Di was looking on, she felt deeply perturbed by the latest turn of events. However, she held different views from those of her host regarding Ole Devil's behavior. Knowing him very well, in spite of their brief acquaintance, she felt sure that he was not acting out of a kind of glory in the *code duello* which caused many young men of his class to issue a challenge to fight under the most flimsy of excuses.

In her summation, the girl was doing less injustice than Turtle to the Texian's motives.

Originally Ole Devil had hoped to arrive in San Phillipe, carry out his business with the hotelkeeper and depart without attracting attention. Due to the intervention of the renegades, there was no longer any hope of doing so. The revelation of Di's identity would, as Trellis's words had proved, be sure to arouse speculation among the customers. Even if they could be prevented from discovering the reason for the visit, knowing who the girl was and the nature of the business with which her family was connected, they would be eager to learn if something of value was being transported in their vicinity.

While Turtle wielded considerable authority in the town, he was not its absolute and unchallenged ruler. Any of the three citizens in the game possessed the means to go against his desires provided they considered there was sufficient inducement. With that in mind, Ole Devil had decided to give them an object lesson. His every instinct warned him that the gambler was posing the most immediate threat. With his curiosity aroused, Trellis would be willing to satisfy it even at the risk of offending the hotelkeeper. Having drawn his conclusion, the young Texian did not hesitate to act upon it.

"There's one thing you'd better know, *nut-man,*" Ole Devil drawled, making no attempt to arm himself. "Down here in Texas, we don't waste time by following the Clonmel Code.* So you can either admit that you accept my word, or pick up that pistol and *try* to use it."

"And have that damned Chink of yours shoot me as soon as I touch it?" Trellis countered, his face's expression ugly in its anger but his inborn caution warning him that he might be approaching a trap.

"With an *empty* rifle?" Turtle commented, darting a glance pregnant with meaning at the other men around the table. He did not say, "He's trying to avoid fighting," but they and the gambler knew it was implied.

"Like hell it's empty!" Trellis spat out, although he guessed that his host was equally aware of the fact. "That thing fires more than one time without reloading."

"The nut-man's right," Ole Devil confirmed, seeing the advantage of allowing his audience to appreciate the Brown-

---

* Clonmel Code: twenty-six "commandments" laying down the rules to be followed when fighting a duel, particularly with pistols, adopted by the Summer Assizes at Clonmel, Tipperary County, Ireland, in 1770.

ing's potential. "But to show that *I* don't need any help, one of you gentleman can cover my man and shoot him if he offers to turn the rifle this way."

"Maybe one of 'em'd best throw down on me, too, Devil," Di suggested, still unaware of why the Texian was determined to force a showdown with the gambler but willing to help. "Seeing's that *hombre's* so all fired scared somebody'll take advantage of him."

"I don't think that *even* Mister Trellis would go that far," Turtle remarked, running a coldly prohibitive gaze at his fellow influential citizens in case any of them should be contemplating taking up Ole Devil's suggestion. "Will your man obey you, Captain Hardin?"

"He will," the Texian declared. "Tommy, take the prisoner and Di's rifle across the room and wait there until I call for you."

"You heard Devil-san," the little Oriental told the captive, tossing down the knife he had been carrying in his left hand and accepting the girl's rifle. "Get going and keep your mouth closed."

Watching Tommy carrying out the first part of the orders, Trellis became aware that other eyes were being turned in his own direction. So he realized that he must decide upon what action to take. Not that he had any real choice. If he backed down, he would be finished in San Phillipe. What was more, he had guessed that only a matter of the greatest importance would bring Di Brindley to the town at that hour of the night. That she was accompanied by a person of Ole Devil Hardin's prominence was further proof of the supposition. If he could dispose of the young Texian, he would be in a better position to satisfy his curiosity. Then, should his belief that the girl's mule train was transporting something of exceptional value be confirmed, he could easily gather sufficient help to take whatever it might be by force.

There was only one problem to be solved.

Disposing of Ole Devil Hardin!

Studying the situation, the gambler felt that he had discovered a way to do it.

"All right," Trellis growled, thrusting back his chair and coming to his feet. "You've asked for it. We'll step outside and I'll give you satisfact—"

In spite of making his suggestion, the gambler had no intention of carrying it out. Not when he had decided that there was a much safer and more certain way to deal with the matter than by facing Ole Devil in a fair fight. Nor would any of the local citizens other than Turtle be inclined to object about his methods. More likely the hotelkeeper's rivals at the table, all of whom had been losers in the poker game, would be only too willing to oppose him. Especially when Trellis had told them of his suspicions over the reason for the girl's arrival.

So, while still speaking, the gambler grabbed for Turtle's pistol. It had been placed barely within reach when he was sitting down and with the barrel pointing toward him. Having stood up had put him even farther from the weapon, but not enough to be detrimental to his chances. The Texian had not made any attempt to arm himself. Nor would he be expecting that there would be any need for him to do so until after they had left the building.

All in all, the scheme appeared sound and certain to succeed.

Unfortunately for Trellis, it was doomed to fail because of his ignorance.

To be fair to the gambler, his error was understandable. While he had been in Texas long enough to have heard of the Brindleys and their business, his only knowledge of Ole Devil had come from Louisiana. Nor had his information been complete.

Even before circumstances had caused Ole Devil to leave the United States, he had developed a very effective method of handling a pistol. While it was not one which would have been permissible under the rigid rules of the Clonmel Code, he had perfected it in the more demanding conditions of his new home.

Alert for treachery, Ole Devil was ready to counter it with deadly efficiency. Turning palm out, his right hand flashed up to coil around the butt of his Manton pistol. In a single motion, he slid the barrel from his belt loop and turned it forward after the fashion gunfighters of a later era would call the "high cavalry twist" draw.* However, unlike the men who would use it in years to come, the shape of his weapon did not permit him to fire one-handed. As he could not cock the hammer with his right thumb, he had trained himself to do it with the heel of his left hand.

Shock twisted at Trellis's face as he was raising the pistol with his left hand on the barrel and the right reaching for the butt. He saw the Texian's weapon was swinging rapidly in his direction and having its hammer cocked at the same time. Then it roared and something which felt like a hot iron bored into the right side of his chest. Slammed backward, agony depriving him of any further conscious thought, he struck the wall and lost his hold on the pistol. Bouncing off, he crumpled and fell.

"Well, gentlemen," Ole Devil said, raking the other participants in the game—apart from Turtle—with coldly menacing eyes. "How do you see it?"

"You did the right thing," the owner of the town's general store declared with only a momentary hesitation. Then, after the other players had stated their concurrence and Turtle's

*A more detailed account of the "high cavalry twist" draw is given in SLIP GUN

men were removing the unconscious gambler, he went on, "Trellis had no call to doubt your word, Captain."

"That wasn't why I called him down and shot him," Ole Devil warned and signaled for Tommy to return with the prisoner. Replacing the pistol in its belt loop, he took back the Browning rifle, continuing, "Most of you are wondering what has brought us here. Trellis guessed that the Ewarts might be moving something of value and had notions of taking it from them. And he was guessing right. They're transporting a consignment for General Houston—and it *is* valuable."

A low hiss of astonishment burst from the girl as she listened, but could hardly believe her ears. From the beginning, Ole Devil had insisted that they must keep their business with Turtle a secret. Yet he was announcing it openly to as mean and ornery a bunch of cutthroats as could be found in —or outside—Texas.

"That's why I forced a fight with him and he's lucky to be alive, I wasn't trying merely to wound him," the Texian elaborated, conscious of Di's restless movements and guessing what was causing them. However, he gave his full attention to the men at Turtle's table while speaking so that his words carried to everybody in the room. "The consignment is so important to General Houston and the future of Texas that anybody with the idea of trying to take it from us had better ask his helpers, 'How many of you want to die?' Because, you have my word on it, that's what any attempt will mean. I've got Company 'C' of the Texas Light Cavalry, fifty strong and fighting men from soda to hock,* backing Ewart Brindley and his Tejas packers. That mule train is going through, gen-

---

* The "soda" and the "hock" were the top and bottom cards of the deck when playing at faro, a description of which is given in RANGELAND HERCULES. So the term "from soda to hock" meant all the way, from the beginning to the end.

tlemen, and I don't give a damn how many I have to kill to
see it reaches General Houston intact."

Studying the grim lines of Ole Devil's Mephistophelian
features and the way in which he stood holding the rifle,
nobody doubted that he meant every word he said.

11
DON'T SHOOT, FELLERS!

"This here's a no good, stupid son-of-a-bitching notion, was you to ask me!" muttered one of the five men who were squatting on their heels in a group under the spreading branches of a big old white oak tree. "Riding all this damned way to lay an ambush for somebody's most likely won't come don't strike me's making real good sense."

"Nor me, neither," declared another member of the quintet, also holding down the level of his voice and darting a glance at a figure which was standing a short distance away. "I don't see nobody's knows sic 'em about Texas being *loco* enough to go to San Phillipe looking for help."

"That's for sure," confirmed a third of the group, speaking no louder than his companions. The mention of the town brought something else to his attention and he went on, "What in hell's keeping Dodd 'n' the others? They sure's hell aren't rushing back, are they?"

Listening to the muted rumble of agreement from the other four men, Madeline de Moreau struggled to keep a check on her normally imperious and demanding nature. Before her husband had been killed by Ole Devil Hardin, the

members of the band of renegades which they had gathered
would not have dared to display opposition to orders in such
an open fashion. Although she felt anger surging through
her, she was aware of her position at that moment, and was
too wise to show it.

Madeline was sufficiently intelligent to appreciate just how
slender a hold she had over the remnants of the band. Serving *Presidente* Antonio Lopez de Santa Anna for profit, as
she and her husband had been, she was all too aware of the
type of men they had enlisted into their organization. Every
one of them had "gone to Texas" to evade the consequences
of criminal activities in the United States of America, and
they were only willing to accept the leadership of a more
ruthless, cold-blooded and dominant personality than their
own. So she had been fortunate in preventing them from
scattering after the fight at the cabin had left her a widow,
and even more so in that they had, albeit reluctantly, agreed
to act upon the plans which she had formulated for making
another attempt to capture the consignment of caplock rifles.
Certainly they did not consider her as the natural successor
to her late husband as head of the band. They had only gone
along with her suggestions out of greed and because nobody
else had been able to think up an alternative scheme.

About five foot eight inches in height and in her early
thirties, Madeline had a full-bosomed, slender-waisted and
curvaceous figure which was not created by artificial aids.
Despite the marks left by her fight with Diamond-Hitch
Brindley—in which she had been coming off a bad second-
best when it was brought to an end—she was a very beautiful
woman. A gray "planter's" hat covered her brunette hair and
her black two-piece riding habit—spare clothing which had
been in her war bag on the cantle of her saddle—was supplemented by the warm man's cloak-coat that she had donned.
Despite her physical attractions, there had always been a

hard and superior air about Madeline which—when they remembered how she and her husband had earned a living
before coming to Texas*—repelled and annoyed the male
members of the band. Nor, feeling nothing but contempt for
what she regarded as the hired help, would she have had it
any other way. As far as she was concerned, even before her
bereavement, they were nothing better than dull-witted, un-
couth animals. Although necessary for Randolph and her
purposes, they were expendable; to be used as long as there
was a need for their services and then discarded. Nor had her
thinking about them changed. Provided things went as she
hoped, she would soon be leaving their company perma-
nently. The kind of life she had been leading recently no
longer had anything to offer, or to hold her in it.

Regardless of her faults, which were many, Madeline had
loved Randolph Galsworthy Buttolph† deeply and sincerely.
Distressed, grieving and enraged by his death, she had sworn
to be avenged upon the man who had killed him. That had
been her main reason for gathering together the men who
had fled from the cabin. Nor could she have hoped to
achieve anything with them, but others of the band—having
been summoned by a message left at one of their hideouts—
arrived. Even with the reinforcements, it had taken all her
persuasive powers before they would agree to carry on with
the task which her husband had started. Nor would she have
succeeded without Dodd's backing. He had always been in-

---

* Before their activities had made the United States of America too hot to
hold them, Madeline and her husband had been actively involved in a white
slavery ring as well as operating a high-class, but notorious, brothel and
gambling house in New York.
† Although Ole Devil Hardin had known Madeline as "de Moreau" and
believed her husband's surname to be "Galsworthy," they were Mr. and
Mrs. Buttolph. However, to avoid confusion, the author will continue to
refer to her by her maiden name, which she and her husband had elected to
use since arriving in Texas.

fatuated by her and had hopes of taking Buttolph's place in
her affections as well as becoming the new leader of the
band.

Conceding that any direct attack upon the well guarded
consignment, or the mule train, was out of the question, the
woman had realized it would become even more difficult to
deal with them after they had come together at Santa Cristóbal Bay. However, Dodd's explanation of how the pack
mules were handled had shown her a way in which she might
be able to attain her desire for profit and revenge. There had
been added inducement in the thought of how the shooting
of Ewart Brindley would affect his granddaughter, for whom
she was nursing a hatred which almost equaled her antipathy
toward Ole Devil Hardin.

Although Madeline would not have been averse to captur-
ing the consignment, that was far from being her primary
consideration. She had been too appreciative of the difficulties involved in taking and disposing of it—as well as retaining the lion's share of the profits it would bring—with her
husband dead to feel sanguine over the chances of success.
So her main objective had been vengeance.

Basing her plan upon a shrewd summation of Ole Devil's
character, formed while in his company as part of her husband's scheme to gain possession of the caplocks, the woman
had guessed how he would respond to the loss of the bell-
mare. Feeling sure that he would personally lead the detail
sent to obtain a replacement, and as he would not wish to
reduce the guards on the consignment or the mules to any
great extent, she knew it would consist of only a few men
despite the unsavory nature of the town's population. She
had argued that catching him would place a useful hostage in
their hands. Even if his men refused to exchange the rifles
for him, or he should be killed, they would be left leaderless
and consequently much easier to deal with.

None of the men, not even Dodd, had suspected Madeline's true motive for bringing them to the San Phillipe area. Being shrewd as well as intelligent, she knew that she could not hope to retain her former position of authority in the band now that her husband was dead. Nor was she willing to act in a subordinate capacity to any other man, particularly those who were with her. So she planned to break away from them and return to the United States, where she felt certain that she could re-establish herself without difficulty, as soon as they had helped her to take revenge upon Buttolph's killer.

On arriving in the vicinity of San Phillipe, Madeline and the men had sought for the best place to establish their ambush. Doing so had only been a matter of selecting the most suitable of several locations, any one of which would have filled their needs adequately. Concluding that their victims would in all probability follow the trail which ran parallel to the coast had made their task easier. However, they had not wanted to be too near to the town in case any shooting that was necessary should be heard and bring some of the citizens to investigate. Being aware of the kind of people who lived there, the renegades had considered it most inadvisable to let them learn about the valuable consignment. With that in mind, they had settled upon a bend with a number of bushes on either side to offer concealment for themselves and their horses. It was in fairly thick woodland and about three miles from the nearest human habitation.

In spite of having agreed to carry out the ambush, a difficulty had arisen. While the men had been willing to take the precaution of eating the food which they were carrying without warming it and to do without lighting a fire, they had started to complain about the lack of liquid refreshment. Finally, to keep the peace, Dodd had taken three companions and set off to purchase a supply of liquor from the town. As he had pointed out to the woman before leaving, some of the others were sure to slip away for it if he did not go and, by taking charge of the party himself, he could make sure that it returned as quickly as possible.

From the way in which her companions had been and still were behaving, Madeline could tell that they were growing less enamored of the scheme. While fine and dry, there was a chill in the air which did nothing to make the waiting more pleasant and comfortable. If the Texian failed to act as she had anticipated, or there should be any other setback, she would lose what little control she had over them. In view of the kind of men they were, especially without Dodd to stand by her, she might suffer an even worse fate than merely being deserted.

"Maybe something's happened to 'em," suggested the fourth of the renegades who were with Madeline on the right side of the trail. "You know what kind of a place San Phillipe is."

"Or it could be they've changed their minds and don't conclude to come back," suggested the man who had started the latest outburst of complaints.

"There's some's wouldn't blame 'em if they have," commented the second speaker. "Hell's teeth, we ain't going to do no son-of-a-bitching good here. Happen Hardin knows about San Phillipe, which 'most everybody in Texas does, he'll not be *loco* enough to come there fixing to get another mare."

"It don't strike me's he would," admitted the last of the quintet.

As the woman heard the trend being taken in the conversation, she began to grow increasingly perturbed. Up to that point, she had drawn some slight comfort from the way in which the men had been speaking. Several feet were separating her from them, which was nothing unusual as she had never mingled closely in their company. Up until that point, she could only just hear their words and had felt sure that they were not aware she could do so. The fact that they were no longer attempting to hold their voices down implied that they might be contemplating a revolt against continuing the ambush.

Worried by the possibility, Madeline slipped her right hand into the side pocket of what had been her husband's cloak-coat. Closing her fingers about the butt of the weapon which was inside, she found herself wishing, not for the first time, that he had had it in his possession when he was confronting Ole Devil Hardin. However, for some reason, he had failed to take the precaution. In view of the latest development, she was not sorry to have it available and unsuspected by her companions. It had a potential which could be of great use if they were considering more than merely deserting her.

Even as the woman was drawing her conclusions, she began to walk in a casual seeming fashion to where her section of the party had left their horses. Although she was alert for any hint that her actions were arousing the men's suspicions, she did not take out the multibarreled Maybury "Pepper-box"* handgun. It offered her the advantage of being able to fire no less than eight shots without needing to be reloaded, but was only .34 in caliber and lacked accuracy at anything except close quarters. If there should be trouble, she planned to stop at least one of her assailants before they were near enough for it to be effective. Her husband had taught her to shoot and she had attained a fair proficiency at it even before her arrival in Texas.

Coming to a halt, as if she had merely gone to check on the animals, Madeline glanced at the group beneath the

* Pepperbox: a multibarreled repeating firearm where all the barrels rotate around an axis instead of, as on a revolver, only the cylinder holding the firing charges.

white oak tree. First one, then another began to stand up and all were gazing in her direction. Alarm and anger gripped her, but not to the extent of rendering her unable to think. The situation was bad, but not desperate. As a precaution in case a hurried departure should become necessary, all the horses were saddled and had the girth tight enough to let them be ridden with the minimum of delay. So she could mount and be gone long before any of them could reach her. Especially if she caused some confusion by shooting one of their number. With that in mind, she lifted one of a brace of pistols from the holsters attached to her saddle's horn. If the men had noticed what she was doing, they made no comment. However, when they heard her drawing the hammer to full cock, they might suspect why she had armed herself.

Even as the woman's left hand went to the hammer, she heard a low whistle from where the sixth member of her group was keeping watch on the trail.

"Hey, Mrs. de Moreau!" hissed the first complainant and, although more softly spoken than his last words, his tones were sullen as he continued, "There's somebody coming!"

Taking advantage of the news as an excuse, Madeline cocked the pistol while returning to the men. They were reaching for rifles, or pistols when the sound of the approaching horses reached their ears.

"Not from the south," the woman said, a touch bitterly. "It's probably only Mister Dodd's party coming back from town."

"It's taken 'em long enough to do it!" commented another of the quintet, just as quietly as the first and sounding equally resentful. "This sitting around waiting's surely hell without a drink to help pass the time."

"I know's I can use one," declared a third speaker, turning toward the trail. "There's no saying how long we'll be here. Or if anybody'll come after we've waited."

With that, the renegade walked in the lookout's direction. Leaving their rifles behind and handguns in their belts, his companions followed. Setting after them, still carrying her pistol, Madeline could see and hear enough to inform her that the other group across the trail were behaving in a similar manner.

Taking the recent events into consideration, the woman was not sorry to hear the approaching riders despite them coming from the wrong direction. While Dodd lacked the masterful personality of her late husband, he was tougher than the others and still a force to be reckoned with in the band. His presence would offer her considerable protection if things should go wrong.

Suddenly a thought struck Madeline and it drove the relief from her mind as she felt sure it had not occurred to any of the men. The riders might not be Dodd's party, but somebody else who had been in San Phillipe and were using the trail. Travelers from the town were likely to be engaged in a way of earning a living which would make them wary and mistrusting. Riding into such a situation, they would be inclined to shoot first and ask questions later.

"Hey there!" yelled a voice, almost quavering with urgency and alarm, to the accompaniment of several bottles clinking against each other, before the woman could put her thoughts into speech. "Don't shoot, fellers! It's only us 'n' we've brought the liquor!"

Having given a startled gasp at the first shouted word, a snort of annoyance burst from Madeline as the explanation continued. From the way in which the approaching rider was carrying on, he considered that he was taking a most sensible and necessary precaution. In fact, his tones suggested that he was very nervous.

For all the woman's relief at discovering the identity of the men on the trail, she silently cursed Dodd for not having kept him quiet. If Ole Devil Hardin—or whoever had been sent to obtain a replacement for the slaughtered bell-mare—was close enough to have heard what was said, he would know that somebody was lurking in the vicinity and ready to start shooting at passersby. While he was unlikely to guess who the ambushers might be, he was certain to take steps to avoid them. Obviously Dodd's party had failed to take that point into consideration. Nor were the rest of the band showing any better grasp of the situation.

"You was right, ma'am!" announced the lookout, no longer bothering to speak quietly. "That's ole Pudsey. I'd know his voice anywheres."

"Sounds like they ain't coming back empty-handed, neither," another renegade went on in normal tones. "Which a drink's what I'm needing right now."

Before Madeline could suggest that they remembered what they had come to try to do, the second speaker started to walk from the bushes and the others followed his example. They were joined by the men from the other side. An ever growing anger filled her as she listened to the commotion her irresponsible companions were making, but she doubted whether they would take any notice if she attempted to make them behave in a more sensible manner. What was more, there was a likelihood that they would become even more noisy. With the mood her group of the ambushers had been in, they could also do worse to her than just alerting anybody who might be in the vicinity of their presence.

A bitter sense of resentment against Dodd began to assail the woman. She wished that he had given more thought to what they hoped to achieve and had restricted the quantity of liquor his party was bringing from San Phillipe. If the clinking was anything to go by, there were sufficient bottles to let them all get drunk and she was all too aware of how dangerous that could be for her. There were men present who had little cause to be kindly disposed toward her. Under the influence of the cheap whiskey, they could decide to repay her for the arrogance she had always shown to them.

Appreciating the peril from the renegades, either if she tried to prevent the issue of the liquor or after they had finished it, Madeline did not follow them. Instead, remaining among the bushes, she peered through the darkness at the four returning members of the band. Although she could only make out their shapes, she concluded from the steady way in which they sat their horses that none of them had imbibed an excessive amount of liquor while they were in town. Clearly Dodd had restrained any desire the other three might have had to overindulge.

Even as the thought came, Madeline grew puzzled. While nowhere near the man her husband had been, Dodd was tough, experienced and not unintelligent. What was more, he had proven himself capable of enforcing his will upon the other members of the band even before he had made his party refrain from getting drunk in San Phillipe.

So why had Dodd allowed Pudsey to call out the warning of their arrival instead of announcing it himself in a more suitable manner?

Or, if it had been done without Dodd's knowledge and authority, why was he keeping silent when he ought to be remonstrating with his indiscreet companion?

With the two points raised, Madeline began to sense that something was very, *very,* wrong. However, for a few seconds, she could not decide what it might be.

Then certain significant, frightening even, factors started to emerge!

Dodd and his companions had all been approximately the same height and build, clad in low crowned hats and range clothes. While the woman could identify the man in the lead as Pudsey, there was considerable disparity between the shapes of himself and two of his companions. What was more, even the fourth of the party—who was behind the other three—struck her as being wrong. After a moment, she realized why.

Pudsey had been marginally the largest of the quartet, yet the man who was following him looked even more massive. In addition, he appeared to have changed his clothes while in the town. At least, there was now a Mexican *sombrero* on his head and he had not been wearing a *serape* when they set off.

Even as Madeline was noticing the fourth rider's change of attire, she became aware of how the horses of the men on either side of Pudsey were behaving. While his mount was walking normally, they seemed restless and reminded her of something. Just what it was struck her an instant later. They looked like a couple of racehorses being restrained, yet ready to hurtle forward when they received the signal to start a race.

Other thoughts crowded into the woman's mind. The rider on the left and slightly behind Pudsey was far smaller than any member of the band.

However, it was the man who was closest to Madeline's position who attracted the majority of her attention. Tall and slender, his right hand hung by his side and the left was also hidden from her view. However, he was sitting his horse with the straight-backed poise which reminded her of an officer in a first-class cavalry regiment riding in a parade.

Or of somebody whom Madeline had come to know—and hate!

With a sensation like an icy cold hand running along her spine, the woman realized what must have happened!

Possibly because Ole Devil Hardin had guessed how she had anticipated his reaction to the shooting of the bell-mare, he had selected a route which had avoided the ambush. In addition, he must have recognized and dealt with Dodd's party in San Phillipe. Pudsey would not hesitate to betray the rest of the band if it would save his own skin.

Suddenly an even greater appreciation of the situation burst upon the woman. Her men were walking toward the riders completely oblivious of their peril. Taken unawares and attacked by three effective fighters, which she did not doubt the Texian's party would be, some of them were certain to be killed.

Apart from one consideration, Madeline would not have worried over what fate had in store for her companions, regarding it as being no more than their stupidity warranted. However, coming in their disgruntled frame of mind, such an event would be all the inducement they needed to flee. Even if she went with them, they would never trust her judgment again. In fact, especially as she could no longer count upon Dodd for protection, they were likely to turn on her and she was all too cognizant with what *that* would mean.

Once again, Madeline was finding her schemes thwarted and her life endangered by the man who had killed her husband!

All the woman's virulent temper erupted!

"It's Hardin!" Madeline shrieked, raising and, confident that she could hit her intended mark, sighting the pistol. Her finger began to tighten on the trigger and she went on, "Kill him!"

12

I'LL NEVER REST UNTIL HE'S DEAD!

Sitting his horse with the reins tied to the saddle horn, but restraining its eagerness to move—by holding the near side ribbon with his pistol-filled left hand—Tommy Okasi watched the renegades. They were emerging from their places of concealment in response to Pudsey's call and the clinking of the empty bottles supplied by Cole Turtle. None of them gave the slightest sign of suspecting that anything was wrong. Even their betrayer's understandably nervous tones had passed unnoticed. As far as the little Oriental could make out, they had left their rifles and were approaching with empty hands. For his part, he was holding his *tachi*—its blade blackened by smoke to avoid any glitter from the steel giving the game away—and the Manton pistol which he had borrowed from his employer. His unstrung bow was suspended in the loops on the left side skirt of his saddle, but he had left the quiver of arrows in Diamond-Hitch Brindley's care.

Studying the situation, Tommy was impressed—as he had been on other occasions—by Ole Devil Hardin's shrewd assessment of human nature. It had already been displayed earlier that night, by the way in which he had turned the events at the San Phillipe Hotel to their advantage.

Despite Tommy's—and, the little Oriental suspected, Di's—original unspoken misgivings as to the wisdom of the Texian's decision to tell the crowd that they were transporting items of considerable value, only good had accrued from it. Supporting his grim warning with a demonstration of his Browning Slide Repeating rifle's potential, by shattering nine bottles in a rapid succession, which would have been beyond the capability of any single shot firearm no matter how well handled, he had increased his audience's awareness that he was a man with whom it would be *very* dangerous to trifle. They had already seen him provoke a fight and cripple one of their number whom he had suspected might pose a threat to the goods in his care. Nor did they doubt that he had sufficient force at his command to back up his statement of intentions.

Always quick to grasp and willing to benefit from any situation, Cole Turtle had reached a decision which was—and would continue to be—of the greatest help to Ole Devil. He had announced that, with the consignment being of such importance to the future of Texas, he meant to do everything in his power to ensure its safe delivery and anybody from the town who attempted to interfere would incur his grave displeasure. All who had heard him knew exactly what he meant.

Having made his position clear, and supported by the hotelkeeper, Ole Devil had turned his attention to the business which had brought them to San Phillipe, and also to removing the threat posed by Madeline de Moreau and her renegades. Once again, Turtle had shown his good faith. In addition to presenting Di with a mare from his stable, he had offered his assistance in dealing with the ambush.

Badly frightened by his predicament, the surviving rene-

gade had done more than tell his captors that his name was
Pudsey. He had described the place where his companions
were waiting. With the added inducement of being told that
he could go free after the ambush had been broken provided
that he got the hell out of Texas by the shortest and quickest
route, he had agreed to lure the rest of the band from where
they would be hiding.

Hearing what the young Texian intended to do, Turtle had
warned that the woman and her party would be expecting
four riders. Although Di had pointed out that she was on
hand to make up the required number, Ole Devil had refused to let her participate. As he had pointed out, if things
should go wrong, somebody had to deliver the mare and
warn Mannen Blaze of what had happened. Once again, Turtle had supplied the answer. Not only had he promised to
give the girl an escort to Santa Cristóbal Bay in such an
eventuality, but he had offered the services of Charlie Slow-
Down to fill the remaining vacancy in the quartet. Di had
reluctantly gone along with Ole Devil's wishes.

Satisfied that he had achieved his original purpose in visit-
ing San Phillipe and, in spite of having failed to keep it a
secret, having prevented the citizens from causing him trouble on account of it, Ole Devil wasted no time in leaving. Nor
had Tommy blamed him for being disinclined to linger any
longer than was necessary in such a location. There was considerable urgency in returning to the mule train with the
replacement bell-mare. What was more, given time, some of
the inhabitants' avaricious natures might override their fear
of opposing Turtle's will. Regaining their courage, they might
start contemplating means by which they could take possession of the consignment.

Once the mare had been handed over to Di and various
other preparations had been completed, Ole Devil, Tommy
and Charlie Slow-Down had set out with Pudsey. Escorted by

Turtle's fifteen-year-old son, Rameses—who was, at a later date, to achieve even greater prominence than his father in the law-breaking circles of Texas*—and four trusted, well-armed men, the girl was following Ole Devil at a safe distance.

When Pudsey had told the Texian that they were drawing close to the curve where the ambush was to take place, the trio had made ready for action. In the Kaddo Indian's case, that had entailed no more than cocking the pair of blunderbuss handguns he was relying upon. Nor had Ole Devil and the little Oriental needed to do much more, but they had a somewhat different problem to contend with. Each was astride a horse trained for cavalry duties. There was only one kind of situation in which such mounts would have their reins fastened to the saddle horn. Their reaction would be to dash forward without any guidance other than the rider's movements on the back, and knee pressure. However, this tendency must be restrained until the most advantageous moment if they were to benefit fully from the element of surprise. So, once the reins had been secured, Ole Devil and Tommy kept hold of one rein with the hand grasping the pistols. These were to augment the swords they were already carrying to ensure that the prisoner did not try to betray them. Although the spirited mounts were restless and eager to move faster, their riders were able to keep them under control, knowing that they would bound forward on being allowed to do so.

Too frightened to be treacherous, even though he was aware of what would happen to at least some of his former companions, Pudsey had carried out his instructions and the perturbed agitation in his voice had failed to warn them that all was far from well. As Ole Devil had hoped, the clinking of

* Some details of "Ram" Turtle's later career are given in SET TEXAS BACK ON HER FEET.

the bottles had drawn the waiting renegades from their places of concealment. What was more, as they walked along the trail, they were not so closely bunched together as to create an extra hazard to what he was planning to do. In fact, they could hardly have positioned themselves more suitably if he had explained what he wanted from them.

However, another problem which the Texian had envisaged had failed to materialize and he did not care for its omission. Sitting his impatient mount, with his right hand held so that his saber—suitably treated like Tommy's *tachi*—was concealed behind his leg, he studied the approaching figures. Although Madeline de Moreau must have been aware of the threat to the ambush, she had made no attempt to halt the exodus of the men from the bushes. Nor could he see her among them. He guessed that she was close by and must be furious at their undisciplined, rowdy behavior.

Measuring the distance separating them from the renegades, Tommy glanced at Ole Devil. Making just as careful an estimate, the Texian decided to hold off until they were a little closer. The nearer they were when they launched their attack, the greater effect it would have and the more damage it would inflict. Nor did he have any qualms over assaulting the men who were walking toward him under the misapprehension that they were approaching friends. In fact, his only regret was that he did not hold a firearm capable of discharging more than one shot, either in succession or as a volley. To have carried his Browning Slide Repeating rifle would have prevented him from using the saber and might have aroused the renegades' suspicions. Nor was there any handgun in production at that time which he felt would have filled his requirements if he had purchased it.*

* *Although the Patent Arms Manufacturing Company was being established by Samuel Colt, with Elias B.D. Ogden (later Judge) as President, and Colt's cousin, Dudley Selden, as Secretary and General Manager, at Pater-*

Although Ole Devil had seen a Collier Repeating Pistol†
on his travels, the fact that it was a flintlock and had more
than forty separate parts in the lock alone—not counting the
lock-plate, attaching screws, stock and barrel-cylinder pin—
in his opinion made it far too delicate and complicated to
handle the work it was now called upon to perform.

Much the same considerations had caused Ole Devil to
reject the various types of multi-barreled "pepperboxes"
which were on sale. None of them, even those designed as
caplocks—particularly as the latter possessed what he regarded as a lethal failing—had struck him as being sufficiently rugged and reliable to stand up to the rigors of conditions in Texas.

However, at that moment and under the prevailing circumstances, the Texian would even have settled for the loan
of the Croodlom & Co. "Duck Foot" Mob Pistol—which
would have allowed him to discharge four .45 caliber bullets
simultaneously and not in the same direction—that Beauregard Rassendyll had brought as a personal sidearm. Such a

---

son, Passaic County, New Jersey, early in 1836 and would receive its charter
on March 5th—and have it amended twice in 1839—it would be another
year before the first of the "Paterson" revolving cylinder rifles and pistols—
the name of the latter becoming shortened to "revolver"—were available to
the public.

† Invented in 1813 by Elisha H. Collier at Boston, Massachusetts. An early
and comparatively successful attempt to create a firearm, utilizing a single
barrel and a hand-operated cylinder rotating with the firing charges, which
could fire several shots in succession. Lack of patronage and production
facilities in the United States of America caused him to cross the Atlantic
and manufacture his arms in England. In spite of Ole Devil's misgivings, a
number of the weapons were purchased for use by the British Army in the
Colonies. Although there is no evidence of the fact, it has been suggested by
some authorities that—having seen examples while serving as a seaman on
a ship which put in at Calcutta, India, then a part of the British Empire—
Samuel Colt, q.v., used the Collier Repeating Pistol as the basis for the
mechanism of his first "revolving cylinder" firearms.

weapon would have served his purpose better than his single-shot Manton pistol.

Ole Devil's yearning for a repeating—or multishot—firearm was not activated by bloodlust, but he refused to be influenced by the knowledge that some of the men before him were going to die without a chance to defend themselves. Not one of them would have hesitated to murder him if they were presented with an opportunity. In fact, some of them had already tried during the fighting at the cabin and they had been waiting in ambush with similar intentions. What was more, some of their number had shot her grandfather, Joe Galton, and the bell-mare while the rest were creating the diversion which had made it possible for them—in part, at least—to achieve their purpose. He knew that they had not even the excuse of patriotism to condone their actions. They were cold-blooded opportunists, traitors to their own kind who were serving a tyrannical dictator for what they could get out of it.

However, revenge was not Ole Devil's primary consideration. First and foremost in his thoughts was the fact that he was up against renegades who were a serious threat to the security of the Republic of Texas. So, he was prepared to be as ruthless as necessary while contending with whoever, or whatever, might be menacing it.

With the latter thought in mind, Ole Devil decided to hold off the attack for a couple or so more yards.

For all that, everything appeared to be going in his party's favor, with the renegades failing to grow alarmed when Ole Devil's party did not answer the shouted greetings. But Ole Devil was perturbed by the woman's absence and silence. Such behavior seemed most unlike her and he wondered where she might be.

Even as the thought came, it was answered in no uncertain manner!

At the first sound of Madeline's voice, which solved the mystery of her whereabouts to the Texian's satisfaction if not relief, he knew that he could not delay the attack any longer.

"Yeeagh!" Ole Devil roared before Madeline had finished speaking, releasing the rein from his left hand and jabbing his heels against his horse's flanks.

"Banzai!" Tommy bellowed at almost the same instant, having duplicated his employer's summation of the situation and giving his mount a similar indication of his wishes.

Unfortunately for Madeline and her companions, the warning she was shrieking—like her realization that the ambush was to be a failure—came just a little too late. Nor did she achieve her intentions by raising the alarm in such a manner. Startled exclamations began to burst from the renegades, but they were not to be granted an opportunity to recover their wits and act upon her advice.

Well trained and knowing what was expected of them, on receiving the awaited signals the two horses lunged forward willingly. The sudden change in the pace of the big dun gelding, to which the Texian had transferred before setting out from Santa Cristóbal Bay, saved its master's life.

Lining her pistol, the woman had completed the pressure on its trigger and the hammer was beginning to fall when the horse obeyed its master's command. Even as the percussion cap was crushed and, in turn, ignited the main charge, she saw her target was passing from in front of the barrel. Nor was there anything she could do to correct the mishap. Being momentarily dazzled by the flames which gushed from the muzzle, she did not see the result of her shot. However, her efforts had not been entirely wasted. She might have missed her intended mark, but the bullet ended its flight in the chest of the man who had betrayed the ambush.

Even as Ole Devil felt the powerful thrust with which the bay responded to his instructions, the sound of the woman's pistol reached his ears to be followed an instant later by the eerie "splat!" which told him that a bullet had passed *very* close behind him. It was succeeded by the unmistakable soggy thud of lead driving into human flesh.

A quick glance to his left satisfied the Texian that the little Oriental was not the woman's victim. He also felt sure that the same applied to Charlie Slow-Down. Judging from the angle the bullets had come, there was only one other alternative, but he did not bother to investigate it. Nothing he had seen of Pudsey caused him to have even the remotest interest in the renegade's well-being.

Not that Ole Devil had the time to ponder extensively upon the identity of whoever it was who had been shot. Almost as soon as he had turned his gaze to the front after checking that Tommy was not the victim, the dun was about to carry him between the foremost of his enemies.

Remembering the advice he had been given by the *maître des armes* who had taught him to wield a saber, Ole Devil did not attempt to slash. Instead, he drove out his weapon with a thrusting motion. Its point entered the mouth of the man on the right, turning his yell of alarm into a strangled gurgle. A moment later, seeming to have responded of its own volition, the Manton pistol boomed awesomely and propelled its ball into the face of the left-hand renegade. The muzzle-blast illuminated Ole Devil's features and its fiery glow made them appear even more Mephistophelian than usual.

Keeping level with his employer, Tommy launched his attack almost simultaneously. Using the point of his *tachi*, he aimed badly and did no more than cut open a man's right shoulder in passing. However, the pistol was more successful and avenged Ewart Brindley by sending its ball into the throat of the man who had shot him.

Pudsey gave a screech of pain as Madeline's bullet found him and he went sideways from the horse. Startled by the commotion, it gave a leap which helped to unseat him and he went crashing to the ground. Nor were his troubles at an end. Alert for the first suggestion that his companions were commencing the attack, Charlie Slow-Down let out a Kaddo war whoop which caused his mount to run. Its hooves struck the injured man as he sprawled helplessly in front of it.

Pandemonium and chaos was reigning unchecked on the trail.

Seeing the pair of riders bearing down upon them, the remaining members of the woman's band made no attempt to draw weapons and defend themselves. Instead, as Ole Devil had anticipated when making his plans for breaking the ambush, they began to scatter so as to avoid their assailants. Not all of them succeeded.

Spinning around, the man who had erroneously reported the return of Dodd's party tried to retire in the direction from which he had come. It proved to be a disastrous choice. Coming up behind him, Ole Devil elevated and brought down the saber in a "cut when chasing" blow which split open his skull and tumbled him lifeless on the trail.

Another renegade might have counted himself more fortunate in that he had been on the left flank of the ambush while waiting for their would-be victims to put in an appearance. Turning and darting toward where his horse was tethered, he went in a direction which kept him clear of the little Oriental's *tachi*. Satisfied that he had escaped death or injury, he continued to flee as fast as his legs could carry him.

Two more of the band were less lucky. Passed by Ole Devil and Tommy, they became the targets for the Kaddo Indian's right-hand blunderbuss. One caught the majority of the sprayed-out lead and the other received a couple of the surplus buckshot balls. Although the latter was injured, he managed to run away. His companion went down, as dead as Dodd had been under similar circumstances.

Within a minute from starting out to greet what they had imagined to be friends carrying liquid refreshment, Madeline de Moreau's band of renegades had ceased to exist as such. Shouting curses, or going in silence and saving their breath, all who could rushed away from the trail with only one aim in mind. To collect a mount and put as much distance between themselves and their assailants as swiftly as possible.

Not that the woman was giving any thought to the disastrous fate into which she had led her male companions. The moment she had realized that Ole Devil Hardin had escaped unscathed from her bullet, she had also known that the time had come to quit their company. Without even waiting to discover how the men might be faring, she lowered the empty pistol and, pivoting on her heels, ran away from the trail.

Reaching her horse, Madeline snatched its reins free from the bush to which it was tied. An excellent rider, she contrived to swing astride the restless animal without relinquishing her hold of the pistol and despite the encumbrance of the cloak-coat. Having done so, she urged it into motion.

From the various sounds to her rear, the woman could tell that her men were not fighting back. So there was no hope that, in some miraculous way, they might turn the tables on their attackers. Any remote chance that they would rally and, possibly, succeed in the purpose of the ambush was dashed by yells of encouragement and the drumming of several horses' hooves originating from the north. Riders coming from that point of the compass were almost certain to be the Texian's friends, particularly as one voice was feminine in timbre and she felt sure she recognized it. Anybody who was accompanying Diamond-Hitch Brindley would only add to the renegades' troubles.

Accepting the inevitable, although she was in a searing rage, the woman guided her horse through the trees at a very fast pace. Furious as she was, she did not ride blindly. Rather the violence of her emotions seemed to increase her perceptions and equestrian skill so that she was traveling much more swiftly than she would have done if she had been in a calmer frame of mind.

Madeline had two objectives as she was allowing her horse to gallop through the woodland.

Firstly, there was the very urgent necessity to get far beyond the reach of the proposed victims of the abortive ambush.

During the time the woman had spent in Di Brindley's and Ole Devil Hardin's company, she had formed a shrewd assessment of their characters. Neither had showed hesitation in risking their lives to ensure the safety of the caplock rifles. So neither would be inclined to show compassion to anybody who had done as much as she to prevent the delivery of the weapons to Major General Samuel Houston and the Republic of Texas's Army. While the Texian *might* be held back from taking extreme measures out of considerations for her sex, the girl most assuredly would not; particularly since the shooting of her grandfather and the pack train's *cargador*.

Secondly and of equal importance, Madeline had no wish to come into further contact with the men she was deserting. After the perilous situation into which she had led them, her fate at their hands would be as bad—probably even worse in some respects—than if the two young people she had been hoping to kill were to capture her. At least, no matter how the girl might wish to act, the Texian would ensure that her end would be quick.

So, while she was riding, Madeline tried to hear if she was being followed. Her instincts warned her that if she was, her pursuers were most likely to be members of her band who were also fleeing from the wrath which had descended upon them. That would not make them any less a menace to her safety. Let them catch up with her and they might shoot her in their rage over their narrow escape from death. However, the noise made by her passage through the woodland prevented her from gaining any information and she had no intention of stopping to listen.

After covering something over a mile in the same reckless fashion, common sense dictated that Madeline should slow down. There was, she realized, a danger that she might ride the horse into the ground if she continued her flight in such a manner. If that happened, she was all too aware of how slim her chances of survival would be.

Taking the sensible line of action, the woman caused her lathered mount to reduce its pace. Struggling to control her own breathing, for riding at a gallop was hard work especially under such demanding conditions, she brought the animal to a halt. She could not hear anything to suggest that the men she had deserted were fighting with their assailants, nor had she expected it. If she knew them, all who were able would already be making good their escape.

Necessity rather than any sense of kindness or responsibility had caused Madeline to become proficient in horse management. So she dismounted and, loosening the girth of her eastern rig, she moved the saddle backward and forward to help cool the animal's back. Having done so, she decided against reloading the pistol—which she had contrived to return to the holster on mounting, leaving her hands free to hold the reins—and resumed her journey on foot.

Violent emotions churned through the woman as, leading the horse by its reins, she walked in a southwesterly direction. She was obsessed by the realization of how close she had been to death, if nothing worse, that night. Instead of admitting that she had brought all her misfortunes on herself, she laid the blame for her past and present predicaments upon the young Texian who had thwarted her and killed the only man she had ever loved.

"Damn Hardin!" Madeline hissed. "I'll never rest until he's dead!"

However, the woman appreciated the difficulties which stood in the way of her quest for vengeance. She could not hope to obtain it unaided. Nor did the answer lie in gathering together such members of the band as had not yet responded to the message left by her late husband at their hideout. They were the same kind of men as those whom she had deserted and she had no desire to put herself in their power.

As far as Madeline could see, there was only one solution. Continue traveling to the south and search for official assistance. She had in her possession a document signed by *Presidente* Antonio Lopez de Santa Anna, demanding that all members of the Mexican Army render her protection or support if either was required. If she could find a unit of suitable strength, its commanding officer would be only too pleased to learn about the consignment of caplock rifles and she might yet bring about the destruction of Ole Devil Hardin. In fact, that would be her price for supplying the information.

13
LOOKS LIKE *YOU* WAS HORNSWOGGLED

"Gott in himmel!" shouted Major Ludwig von Lowenbrau, commanding Company "B" of the Red River Volunteer Dragoons, as the rising sun allowed him his first unimpeded view into the hollow which surrounded Santa Cristóbal Bay. In the stress of his emotion, he continued to speak with his native tongue. "If I'd known last night—"

Realizing that there were some of his subordinates also studying the terrain and its occupants below, von Lowenbrau made an almost visible effort to restrain his display of anger and surprise. It would never do for them to suspect, even if they had not understood his words, just how badly he had been mistaken in his summation of the situation. Discipline in his regiment was slack enough without him behaving in a manner likely to increase their disrespect. However, while outwardly he resumed his hard and expressionless demeanor, internally he was boiling with rage and mortification.

No man, particularly a proud and arrogant former Prussian officer who also considered himself a capable gambler, enjoyed learning that he had been tricked. Yet, taking in the sight which was spread beneath him, von Lowenbrau knew that he had fallen for a bluff. Realizing who was responsible for it did nothing to improve his feelings.

It was, the major concluded bitterly, all too easy to be wise *after* the event!

Everything about the previous night had suggested that von Lowenbrau might be leading his men into a situation which they could not handle and from which they were likely to suffer heavy losses. From all appearances, his purpose had been suspected, and very effective measures taken to circumvent it. The disparity between the references made by Mannen Blaze and the sentry regarding Ole Devil Hardin's whereabouts had suggested that he was close at hand instead of being away relieving the pickets. Such would have been a task assigned to a subordinate, for it did not require the services of the company's commanding officer. Of course, Hardin might have been reluctant to trust it to such an incompetent second-in-command, but he would have been even more reluctant to leave Blaze in charge of the consignment of caplocks.

All in all, von Lowenbrau had been convinced that there was too much organization about his reception for it to have been arranged by Hardin's dull-witted lieutenant. So, he had decided it was wise not to enter the hollow. And Blaze's mention of yellow fever made his men unwilling to approach the source of such a virulently infectious disease.

Having been well trained in an officer's duties, von Lowenbrau had decided to wait for daylight to reassess the situation and form a better impression of it. Once he had seen the exact strength of the opposition, he could estimate the chances of being able to carry out his assignment by force if necessary.

With that in mind, the major had ordered his company to make camp on the rim. Although Blaze had withdrawn the majority of his men, he had left two sentries at the top of the slope. Nor had there been a time when they, or their reliefs, relaxed their vigilance and most of it had been directed at the Prussian and his subordinates. However, much to his surprise, they had rejoined their companions as soon as his men had shown signs of rising.

Dawn's gray light showed von Lowenbrau just how he had been misled!

One of the first things to strike the major on commencing his examination was the absence of Ewart Brindley's mules. He had wondered why the animals were so quiet during the night and had finally concluded that, having been pushed hard on the journey to the bay, they were sleeping.

However, the matter of the missing mule train struck von Lowenbrau as being a minor issue. Once he had taken charge of the consignment, he would wait until Brindley arrived and then commandeer the animals for his own use. From what he could see, gaining possession of the caplocks would not be as difficult as he had anticipated.

On counting the men in the hollow, von Lowenbrau found there were nowhere near as many as he had anticipated. In fact, his contingent had the consignment's guards outnumbered by close to three to one. However, Hardin's men—although he did not appear to be present—were ensconced in pits which had been sited so as to offer protection against assailants who were descending from the rim. Each of them had no less than five rifles close at hand.

"Looks like *you* was hornswoggled, *Major,*" remarked Lou Benn, a burly and sullen featured man who held rank as sergeant and had ambitions to become an officer. He had given the situation a similar evaluation and drawing much the same conclusions as the Major. "What're *you* fixing to have us do now?"

The words came to von Lowenbrau like the thrust of a sharp-roweled spur. All too well he could imagine how the story of his failure would be received if they returned empty-handed to the regiment. There were many, including the speaker, who hated him and would be delighted to see him humbled. In fact, the colonel might even use it to remove him from his position of command.

"Have the men saddle up," the major ordered, goaded by the need to take some kind of action and thinking about the consequences of going back a failure. "We're going down for the rifles and ammunition."

"Ole Devil Hardin's not the man to give—" Benn began.

"Hardin's not there!" von Lowenbrau pointed out, snapping shut the telescope through which he had been conducting his scrutiny. "And, even if he was, I outrank him. So saddle up, damn you. We have them outnumbered and, as they've only got Blaze in command, there won't be any trouble from them."

While the sergeant felt that his superior might be somewhat overconfident, he did not announce his misgivings. Fancy-dressed and high-toned the Prussian—like many of his race, he grew indignant if called a German—might be, but he had gained the reputation for being bad medicine when crossed. What was more, Benn had to concede that he had been correct on two points.

Firstly, the numerical odds were well in the Dragoons' favor.

Secondly, as far as Benn could make out—and he too had used a telescope to look *very* carefully—Ole Devil Hardin was not present. One did not easily forget such a man and the sergeant was confident that he could have made the required identification if its subject had been available.

Sharing von Lowenbrau's low opinion of Mannen Blaze's personality and capability, Benn also considered that it would be possible to commandeer—he disliked the more accurate term "steal"—the consignment. The Texas Light Cavalry's enlisted men were unlikely to resist with their commanding officer absent and while they were being led by a numbskull who acted most of the time like he was about to fall asleep. Especially when they found themselves confronted by a determined force of nearly three times their numbers.

Nor, if it came to a point, did the sergeant relish the notion of reporting to Colonel Johnson without having successfully accomplished the mission. He had his eyes set upon promotion to and the status—plus benefits—gained by being an officer. So delivering the caplocks would be a big step toward attaining his ambition. Turning, he barked orders which sent the rest of the Dragoons hurrying to saddle their horses.

"Bring the pack animals too," von Lowenbrau commanded. "I want every man going down there with us."

"Here they come, Mannen," Beauregard Rassendyll remarked, looking at the rim and wishing he could draw the sword he was wearing to supplement the Croodlom & Co. "Duck Foot" Mob Pistol which dangled in his right hand. However, the burly redhead had said that he must not and— no matter what his earlier opinion of the other had been— the events of the previous night had made him willing to bow to what he now accepted as superior wisdom. "And, was I asked, I'd say they were ready to make trouble."

"Yep," Mannen Blaze conceded, still sounding as if he might fall asleep at any moment. Standing by the supercargo, with the Browning Slide Repeating rifle across the crook of his left arm, he studied the approaching riders as they spread out to descend the slope in line abreast. "They're loaded for b'ar, not squirrel, I'd say."

Which was, the burly redhead told himself silently, pretty well what he had expected would happen once Major Ludwig

von Lowenbrau discovered the exact strength—or lack of it
—of the force at his disposal.

There were, Mannen conceded, a few consolations. His
ruse and the intelligent backing of the men under his command had bought him some valuable time. Unless Smith—
who had been replaced by another sentry on the rim—had
been prevented from departing, help should already be on its
way from the mule train.

The big question was, would it arrive in time?

Mannen had hoped that the reinforcements would have
put in an appearance before von Lowenbrau could find out
that he had been tricked. Unfortunately, the hope had not
materialized. Nor, from what Mannen could remember of
the major, would he be likely to turn aside after he had been
seen by his men to have fallen for a bluff. In fact, going by
the way each of his men was nursing a rifle, it had made him
even more determined to carry out his intentions—

And a man did not need to be a mind reader to work out
what they must be!

Sweeping a quick glance at the few members of Company
"C" who were at his disposal, Mannen could find no traces of
alarm and despondency as they watched the thirty or so
Dragoons. He did not doubt that they were ready and willing
to fight despite the disparity of their numbers, but that was a
mixed blessing. Even if they should be victorious, he could
imagine how the rest of the Republic of Texas's Army would
react to the news—which was sure to leak out—that two
outfits had done battle with each other. Morale was low
enough already without giving Major General Samuel Houston that sort of a situation to contend with.

"Don't any of you make what could be called a hostile, or
even threatening, move," Mannen warned, in tones more
suggestive that he was complaining over having had a nap

disturbed and which fooled none of his audience. "And stay put in those holes you volunteered to dig."

"That was volunteering?" asked one of the enlisted men, with a grin, for the redhead had insisted that the pits were dug as a precaution the previous evening.

"You 'n' Mister Rassendyll get into your'n *pronto* comes trouble, Mister Blaze," Sergeant Dale requested, after the chuckles had ended, for the two young men alone were standing exposed to their visitors. "We'd hate for him to get killed afore we've seen if that danged thing he's holding really can shoot."

"I'll do my best not to disappoint you, Sergeant," Rassendyll promised, delighted by the evidence that his status had improved where his comrades-in-arms were concerned.

Up until the supercargo's collection and use of the bull's-eye lantern the previous night, he had been annoyed to find that the Texians did not hold him in very high esteem. Partly it had been his own fault. His earlier attitude was not calculated to be acceptable to such fiercely independent souls. So his assumption that he would automatically be accorded the same respect as Ole Devil and Mannen had antagonized them. However, having demonstrated that he was good for something more than dressing fancy, handling the easiest part of the consignment's delivery, and toting a mighty peculiar kind of handgun, he was being treated as an equal.

Conscious of his companion's elation, Mannen did not allow it to distract him. Instead, he continued to keep the Dragoons under observation and waited to see what would develop. He felt satisfied that he had done everything he could to receive them.

"Halt the men here, Sergeant!" von Lowenbrau ordered, while a good fifty yards still separated them from their objective.

"Huh?" grunted Benn.

"You heard!" the major snarled, glancing back and finding that the men were already obeying without the non-com's orders. "Come up when I signal."

Riding onward, von Lowenbrau studied the Texians. Noticing the disciplined manner in which they were behaving, he could not help wishing that the Red River Volunteer Dragoons could be counted upon to act in such a fashion. However, he put the thought from his mind. Bringing his horse to a stop about thirty feet from the closest rifle pit, he dismounted.

"Your men seem to have recovered rapidly, Mister Blaze," the major commented dryly, leaving the animal and walking —marching in review would be a better description—forward.

While advancing, von Lowenbrau studied Rassendyll and made an accurate guess at his reason for being present. Briefly, the Prussian wondered if he had been the brains behind the preparations and bluff. It was possible, but for one thing. All too well, from his own experiences shortly after his arrival in Texas, von Lowenbrau knew the ruggedly individualistic spirit of the colonists. They would never have accepted the leadership of a newcomer in such a short time.

"Must have only been a touch of the grippe, Major," Mannen replied blandly. "Anyways, they're over it now, no matter what it was, so I'm giving them a mite of training to stop them thinking about it."

"Is this your entire command?" von Lowenbrau demanded.

"The rest of them are off someplace with Cousin Dev— Captain Hardin," Mannen replied, looking and sounding exceptionally somnolent. "They *should* be back some—any time now."

"And until they return, this valuable consignment of arms

has been left with completely inadequate protection!" the Prussian barked, barely able to restrain himself from bellowing at the redhead to wake up. Then he glanced at Rassendyll as if expecting some comment. When it did not come, he continued, "That won't do. I'll take it in my charge."

"Well now, Major," Mannen drawled and, although he seemed to be finding it difficult to stay awake, he sounded both grateful and perturbed. "Grateful as I am for you offering, I couldn't rightly let you do that."

"I'm not making a friendly *request,* mister!" von Lowenbrau warned, still wondering why the other young man did not intervene. "I'm ordering you to hand it over."

While speaking, the major made a beckoning motion with his lowered left hand. Seeing the signal, Benn growled at the Dragoons to advance. However, conscious of the menace from the rifles of the soldiers in the pits, he held the pace to a walk and issued a warning that nobody had to even look like raising a weapon.

"Isn't there some rule or other's calls it mutiny if I don't obey an order from a superior officer?" Mannen inquired worriedly, raising his eyes to look at the approaching Dragoons as if wishing to avoid meeting the Prussian's gaze.

"There is," von Lowenbrau confirmed with grim satisfaction, deciding that his task was growing easier. "And the punishment for mutiny is death."

For all his feeling that the burly redhead would yield to his demand, the major became conscious of how the men in the rifle pits were reacting. None seemed alarmed, or disturbed by the sight of his Dragoons riding nearer. Instead, they seemed to be finding the affair interesting and even amusing. There was something vaguely familiar about their attitudes, but he was unable to decide what it might be.

"And so, Mister Blaze," von Lowenbrau went on, as Benn

brought the Dragoons to a halt near his horse, "I am ordering you to hand over the consignment to me. If you refuse, I will have to regard it as an act of mutiny and you will suffer the consequences."

14

I CAN REPAY YOU FOR SAVING ME!

Without realizing that some six miles to the northeast another threat had arisen to the safety of the consignment of arms which had caused her husband's death, tiredness and the knowledge that she must allow her horse to rest brought Madeline de Moreau to a halt.

Once her mount had recovered its breath after the mad dash through the woodland, the woman had mounted and pushed on with all the speed she could muster. Using the training she had received from her husband, she had continued to travel southwest. While she had known that the most simple way to find members of the Mexican Army would be to follow the coast road, she had also seen the objections to doing so. The trail did not go into Santa Cristóbal Bay, but went sufficiently close to it for there to be the danger of meeting with pickets set out by Ole Devil Hardin before he had left for San Phillipe. He was too intelligent, damn him, to have overlooked such a precaution.

What was more, before Madeline could reach territory under Mexican control, she would have to pass areas occupied by other Texian outfits. Probably they would not molest her, but she would be expected to give an account of her presence and had no wish to attract such undesirable attention. There was no way in which she could be sure that Hardin had not passed word of her activities. It would not have surprised her if he had. So she was disinclined to take the chance.

So Madeline had kept moving across country. It said much for her physical condition that she had got so far during the hours of darkness. Furthermore, she might have counted herself fortunate that she was such a skilled horsewoman and astride an exceptionally reliable mount. Exhausted by the strain which she had been under, she had found herself repeatedly threatened with dropping off to sleep as she was riding. In fact, she had been dozing and almost fallen from the saddle before she woke up and, taking the warning, concluded that she must grab some rest.

Gazing ahead with eyes glazed by fatigue, the woman located a place where she could satisfy her craving for sleep. The terrain was once more fairly dense woodland, with plenty of undergrowth. However, she was approaching a clearing through which a small stream was flowing.

If Madeline had been in a more alert frame of mind, she might have heard and been alarmed by certain noises from not too far behind her. Barely able to keep her eyes open, she was only conscious of one thing. That she had found a reasonably safe haven in which she could rest.

Entering the clearing and finding it deserted, the brunette allowed her horse to reach the bank of the stream before halting it and dismounting. Its pace had been slow enough for the last hour for it to be able to drink without harmful effects. Removing the bit, she allowed it to do so.

In spite of her tiredness, Madeline knew that there were things which she must do before she dared to succumb to sleep. First, she had to make sure that her mount would still be available when she woke up. Removing the cloak-coat, she laid it on the ground without removing the "Pepperbox" from its pocket. Then she took a set of hobbles from her saddle pouch and applied them to the pasterns* of the animal's forelegs. With that done, she removed the rig. There was one more essential task to be attended to, she told herself, and she would do it as soon as she had set her burden down.

"Well dog my cats, Nippy, you was right," declared a hard masculine voice, coming from the bushes through which the woman had passed on her way into the clearing. "It air that high-toned Mrs. dee Moreau."

"Only she don't look nowheres near's high-toned now as when her and that stinking mac was treating us like dirt," answered a second set of male tones. "Nor when her damned fool notions was getting some of the boys killed."

Letting the saddle slip from her fingers, Madeline stared at the speakers. Even if she had not recognized their voices, the words would have informed her that they were members of her husband's band of renegades. Not that she took any pleasure from finding them striding toward her. Rather the opposite. In addition to insulting his memory by referring to Randolph as a "mac," which meant a pimp, they had been two of the more vocal malcontents in her party before the disastrously abortive ambush. Nor, judging from their comments and expressions, were they coming with friendly intentions.

Bending, the woman snatched the upper of the brace of pistols from the holsters on her saddle horn. Knowing how capable she was, the men started to run toward her. Even as her brain began to scream a warning, she cocked and raised the weapon to aim at Nippy. However, although she realized the futility of the gesture, she could not stop herself from snatching at the trigger. The hammer fell, but there was only

*Pastern: part of the horse's leg immediately above the hoof.

a click. In her haste, she had selected the pistol with which she had tried to kill Ole Devil Hardin.

Letting out a shriek of combined rage and fear, Madeline flung the empty weapon at Nippy. She missed, but was already grabbing for its mate when she saw each man's face registering alarm and fright.

Something passed through the air close above the woman and struck Nippy between the eyes with considerable force. His head snapped to the rear and he pitched over backward. Bouncing off after the impact, the missile proved to be a sturdy piece of curved wood.

An instant after the renegade was hit, there was a different kind of hiss and the second man, trying to stop running, gave a convulsive jerk. With his hands rising to claw ineffectually at the fletching of the arrow which had buried itself in his chest, he spun around and collapsed.

Looking over her shoulder with her fingers closing on the butt of the loaded pistol, Madeline did not know whether to be pleased or terrified. While they had rescued her from the renegades, her fate at the hands of the two Indians across the stream might not be different from that which Nippy and his companion had intended. It could, however, result in a quicker death. Nippy's killer no longer held a weapon, but the second brave was already reaching for another arrow from his quiver.

"Don't kill her!" yelled a voice in Spanish.

Another man appeared, striding from behind a bush. At the sight of him, Madeline straightened up without drawing the pistol. Although she did not know to which regiment he belonged, the newcomer was an officer in the Mexican Army. His black busby, which had lost part of its Quetzal's tail feathers' plume, and light green Hussar-type uniform suggested he served in a volunteer unit. There was an air of breeding about him which she found comforting. Such a man would be more willing to honor her identification pass from *Presidente* Antonio Lopes de Santa Anna than either of the Indians.

"Gracias, señor," Madeline said, also employing Spanish. "I can repay you for saving me."

Five minutes later, Major Abrahan Phillipe Gonzales *de* Villena *y* Danvila of the Arizona Hopi *Activos* Regiment had solved the mystery which had brought him back accompanied by a small party of braves who had been sent to locate him. He knew why two members of the Texas Light Cavalry were so far from their regiment's last reported position.

"Dang it all!" Mannen Blaze almost wailed, in a sleepily petulant tone, after Major Ludwig von Lowenbrau had delivered the ultimatum. "It looks like one way or the other I'm forced and bound to become a mutineer and get shot. Because Captain Hardin, who's my superior officer, *ordered* me to hold on to the consignment until he comes back."

"Damn it, man," the Prussian thundered, all his military background and upbringing revolting at such a display of stupidity from an officer. "I'm a major and that's senior to a captain. So, in Captain Hardin's absence, I'm countermanding his order and assuming authority for—"

"Excuse me for interrupting, Major," the redhead put in, exuding a slothfully apologetic aura. "But before you can countermand an order in Captain Hardin's absence, he had to be absent—doesn't he?"

"Of course—!" von Lowenbrau commenced, before he could stop himself. "What do you mean, damn it?"

"It's just that I can't see how he can be absent," Mannen explained, "when he's walking down the slope behind you."

Looking over his shoulder, the Prussian let out a guttural and explosive oath in his native tongue. Unnoticed by the rest of the Red River Volunteer Dragoons' contingent, three men were advancing on foot and had almost reached them.

Von Lowenbrau recognized all the trio. At the right, carrying a strange-looking rifle, was the man who had departed during the night. Apparently he had partly told the truth about his reason for going. On the left, with an arrow nocked to the string of the remarkably long bow he was carrying and armed with two swords, was Hardin's "Chinese" servant.

However, the Prussian's main attention was focused upon Tommy Okasi's employer. Unshaven, showing signs of having ridden hard and fast, clearly very tired, Ole Devil Hardin still contrived to stride out with a smart, almost gasconading, swagger. Unlike his escort, he had no weapon in his hands.

Suddenly, von Lowenbrau realized what the attitudes of the Texians in the rifle pits had reminded him of. It had been the look of men who knew that somebody they disliked was shortly to be given an unpleasant shock. Obviously they had seen their captain coming even though their other officer had not.

Or had Mannen Blaze been aware of his cousin's arrival?

Considering the behavior of the man who had accompanied the consignment from New Orleans and who had remained silent when he should have been protesting or trying to take control from the bumbling, incompetent redhead, the Prussian was puzzled. Either the burly lieutenant had been exceptionally lucky, or he was far from the dullard he appeared.

However, there was no time for von Lowenbrau to ponder on the question. Glancing at the rim, he stiffened. There were several men armed with rifles advancing from it. They had not been there when he had led his Dragoons into the hollow. The members of his company were not yet aware of the new and very dangerous factor which had arisen.

"Good morning, Captain Hardin," the Prussian greeted,

hoping that none of his Dragoons did anything stupid. While the man he was addressing kept walking, the other two had halted to their rear. "I'm pleased to see that you have brought more men to help guard the consignment."

"Good morning, Major von Lowenbrau," Ole Devil replied, knowing that the second sentence had been a warning to the Dragoons, but he passed without as much as a glance in their direction.

On arriving at the mule train, having found Smith there and learning of Mannen's problem, the Texian had wasted no time. Borrowing fresh mounts, he, Tommy, Smith and fifteen members of Sergeant Maxime's detail had set out to give support to his cousin. Reaching the vicinity just as the major was leading the Dragoons into the hollow and realizing that they were unaware of his party's presence, he had gambled upon Mannen being able to keep the Prussian occupied until he was ready to take over. From all appearances, the redhead had—as on other occasions—fully justified his cousin's faith in him.

"Anything to report, Mister Blaze?" Ole Devil asked, halting in between von Lowenbrau and the Dragoons, but looking by the major and still ignoring his men.

"Everything's set up ready for moving as soon as the mules arrive, sir, except for the rifles you told me to have loaded and held in reserve in case of an emergency," Mannen reported, with slightly greater animation than he had shown so far and using the honorific which he had not employed when addressing the Prussian. "The major was good enough to have his men stand watch last night, so I called in our sentries."

"*Bueno,*" Ole Devil praised, then turned his attention to von Lowenbrau. "Thank you, Major. The safety of this consignment is of the greatest importance."

"You seem to have been taking its safekeeping lightly," the

Prussian answered. "I arrived to find you absent and your second-in-command with insufficient men to ensure its protection. If that's—"

"Damn it—!" Beauregard Rassendyll shouted, filled with indignation at such an unjust criticism of his friend.

"You're at attention, Mister Rassendyll!" Ole Devil interrupted, without taking his eyes from von Lowenbrau. "It appears that they've protected it adequately regardless of their numbers, Major. May I ask what brings you hereabouts?"

"I've been sent to take charge of this consignment," von Lowenbrau replied.

"On whose orders?"

"*Colonel* Frank Johnson's. He has given me written authority—"

"With respect, sir," Ole Devil put in, although his tones were far from apologetic, "my orders come from *Major General* Houston. They are that I'm to deliver the arms to him and, unless I receive *written* instructions to the contrary from *him*, that's exactly what I intend to do."

There von Lowenbrau had it, just as plainly as anybody could have asked for.

Being close enough to hear the conversation, the Dragoons waited—the majority with bated breath—to discover what their officer meant to do. They were not unmindful of the danger to themselves if he tried to enforce his demand. While outnumbering the contingent from the Texas Light Cavalry, they offered a better target to the men in the rifle pits than vice versa.

"The primary purpose of an officer is to obey his superior's orders, *Captain* Hardin!" von Lowenbrau pointed out, sharing his men's awareness of the situation and playing for time in the hope that he might find a way to gain ascendancy over the tall, ramrod straight young Texian. One thing was for sure, unlike his cousin, he would not be frightened by the prospects of committing mutiny by refusing to obey.

"Yes, sir," Ole Devil replied, chopping off the other's thought train. "Which is why the Texas Light Cavalry and other regiments are withdrawing to the east as General Houston ordered."

Just as the Texian had anticipated, from what he remembered of von Lowenbrau's character from their meetings, the comment was not well received. No matter what had caused the Prussian to have "gone to Texas," he still retained much of the training which was instilled since his early childhood. *"Befehl is befehl,"* orders are orders, was the creed by which he had been raised. So he had never been completely reconciled to serving Johnson. He was honest enough to admit to himself that loot rather than patriotism, or even strategy, was the main purpose behind the proposed invasion of Mexico. What was more, it went against the commanding general of the Republic of Texas's Army's policies and instructions.

"And what does *that* mean?" von Lowenbrau demanded, his face struggling to remain as impassive as Ole Devil's Mephistophelian features.

"Looky here now!" called the Dragoons' sergeant, seeing what he regarded as his opportunity and appreciating how his words would sound when reported to their superiors on rejoining the regiment. "All this talk's fine, but it ain't getting us them rifles."

"You're not having them, *hombre*!" Ole Devil stated flatly, turning to face the speaker and seeing how he might turn the interruption to his advantage.

"Now you just listen to me!" Sergeant Benn growled, the Texian's obvious disdain causing him to forget that the odds were no longer in his company's favor. "We've been told by Colonel Johnson to take 'em and that's what *I'm* fixing to do."

"You are?" Ole Devil challenged, noticing that the Prussian was not offering to intervene and, while guessing why, pleased that he had not.

"Me 'n' these fellers here," Benn corrected, having understood the implications of the Texian's emphasis on the word *"you"* but oblivious of the consternation being shown by the majority of "these fellers here."

"You'll have to kill all of *us* first," Ole Devil warned. "And we'll try to stop you. And we're in a better position to stop you than you are to kill us."

"You don't reckon's them boys back of you'd throw lead us's is good 'n' loyal Texians same's them," Benn countered. "Now do you?"

"Hombre!" Sergeant Dale called, before his superior could reply. "We'd throw lead at our own mothers happen Cap'n Hardin gave the word and we knowed he was in the right."

"Which we-all concludes he's in the right just now," announced a grizzled old-timer from another pit.

"So, happen you jaspers want it," went on the youngest member of Company "C," in the belief that he too would be helping out, "just come on ahead and try to take it from us."

While Ole Devil had been delighted by the first two comments, he was less enamored of the third remark. It was too like a direct challenge and there looked to be a few equally young hotheads among the Dragoons who, despite their companions' appreciation of the danger, would want to pick up the gauntlet. If that happened, blood was sure to flow and, like Mannen, he was equally aware of the subsidiary consequences of such a fight.

"There's no call for men who're needed to help fight Santa Anna to get killed," the Texian pointed out, still keeping his gaze on Benn. "If *you*'re so set on having the consignment, *hombre, I'll* fight *you* for it."

"What—?" gasped the sergeant, conscious of the muted rumble of conversation to his rear.

"It should be plain enough, even for *you*," Ole Devil replied dryly, walking forward. "If *you* can kill *me, just us two, nobody else* involved, Mister Blaze has my orders to give it to you."

"Stay put, Major," advised Mannen, as von Lowenbrau began to move. "You've let it get this far, now see it through. That way, a whole slew of lives will be saved."

Assessing the redhead's comment and the situation with a gambler's cool calculation rather than an officer's training, the Prussian knew he was hearing the truth. Having set the stakes in the game, Hardin would have to face the consequences. If he lost, his own men would insist that the forfeit be paid. So von Lowenbrau stood still, allowing the events to run their course without his participation.

As with the case of most of his regiment's non-coms, the sergeant had been promoted through his connections and toughness rather than military qualities and intelligence. However, he was smart enough to duplicate his superior's summation of how his victory would be received.

And Benn also knew that there was only one way in which the prize could be won!

Studying the man who had made the offer, the sergeant found that he did not care for what he was seeing.

Although Ole Devil had never heard the term, he appreciated the psychological effect produced by his hornlike hairstyle and features in times of trouble. So he had shoved back his hat and allowed it to dangle on his shoulders by its *barbiquejo*. Unshaven, haggard from lack of sleep, even without the savage challenge that it bore, his face had never appeared more Satanic.

To Benn, whose childhood religious instruction had instilled a hearty fear for the possible wrath of the hereafter—although it had been many years since he last saw the inside of a confession box—it seemed that he was confronted by Old Nick himself all ready, willing and out-and-out eager to pitchfork him into a fiery furnace.

"Let's take—" the sergeant began, just managing to control a desire to make the sign of the cross as he had been taught by the Fathers and looking to his rear in the hope of enlisting support.

"This is between just you and I, *hombre!*" Ole Devil snapped, bringing the other's head to the front and ending his words. "So either get down from that horse and make your play, or turn it and ride out of this hollow."

"But—" Benn commenced, staring as if mesmerized at the Mephistophelian face.

"Count to five, Mister Blaze," Ole Devil ordered, still staring with awesome intensity at the sergeant. "And, *hombre*, if you haven't done one or the other by the time it's reached, I'll kill you where you sit."

"One!" Mannen said, as soon as his cousin had stopped speaking.

"Hey now—" Benn growled, realizing the position in which he had been placed.

"Two!" Mannen went on unhurriedly, but ignoring the interjection.

While the redhead was counting, he knew without needing to be told what his cousin wanted. So he did not hurry his words. While Mannen did not doubt that Ole Devil would carry out the threat, he guessed that the other would prefer that the need to do so did not arise. So he intended to give the sergeant time to back off.

Waiting for the count to continue, Benn considered his position faster than he was used to thinking. On the face of it, he held the advantage. His rifle lay across his knees, not yet cocked but more available than any weapon carried by the empty-handed young man in front of him. However, even as he was on the point of turning the barrel forward, doubts began to assail him.

Would Hardin be taking such a chance unless he was completely confident of surviving?

Knowing that he personally would not, the sergeant based his answer upon his own standards.

If the young Texian had accepted the risk when making the challenge, he must be certain that he would win!

"Three!" Mannen drawled, seeing the perturbation on the sergeant's face.

Would Hardin kill another member of the Republic of Texas's Army?

Ben did not doubt that, under the circumstances, the answer was "yes!"

"Four!"

Inexorably, if unhurriedly, the count was going on!

Standing as rigidly as if waiting to be inspected by the Emperor of Prussia, von Lowenbrau watched and waited without offering to intercede. Like his sergeant, he felt certain that Ole Devil would carry out the threat. Faced by something which was endangering the consignment he had been entrusted to deliver and aware that it might make all the difference when the time came for the Texians to make their stand against Santa Anna's Army, he would deal ruthlessly with anybody who tried to stop him.

As far as von Lowenbrau could see, he stood to benefit in one of two ways dependent on the result. Should Benn succeed, the consignment would be in their hands and his own moral dominance would soon put him back in full command of the company. If Hardin won, he would be rid of a troublesome subordinate who was too well connected in the regiment for his demotion or removal in any other way.

For his part, Benn had been counting upon the backing of the other Dragoons, but he now knew that it would not be forthcoming. So he would have to stand—or fall—alone.

Suddenly the sergeant experienced a sense of overwhelming fear. The motionless figure with the face of the Devil was something beyond his comprehension. Despite his empty hands, he seemed as grimly inevitable as death and just as permanent. Although he was making no attempt to arm himself, the sergeant knew that somehow he had the means to do what he had said he would.

Seeing Mannen's mouth starting to open for what would be the last digit of the count, Benn's courage—always more bravado than bravery—broke. Reining his horse around and dropping his rifle, he rode up the slope at an ever increasing pace.

"Don't you say a word!" Sergeant Dale snarled at the youngest member of Company "C," who was on the point of making a derisive comment, and his order was obeyed.

Von Lowenbrau watched his ex-sergeant's flight with mixed emotions. Two things he knew were sure. After such behavior, Benn was through. However, having seen the noncom routed, the rest of the Dragoons would refuse to attempt anything he wanted to try and carry out the assignment.

"Any of you who want to go with him may do so," the Prussian announced, raking his men with cold eyes. "Whoever stays will ride with me."

"Where are you going, Major?" Ole Devil inquired, turning to look at the speaker.

"With you, if you let me, Captain," von Lowenbrau replied. "My men and I may be of assistance until you've delivered the arms to General Houston."

"How about Colonel Johnson?" Ole Devil asked.

"I'm going to serve a better man," the Prussian stated. "And we'll be riding in better company than any under Johnson's command. If *you'll* permit us to accompany you that is."

15
I'LL COME AND HOLD YOUR HANDS

Old Devil Hardin had an active and inquiring mind which would always take an interest in anything he believed might one day be of service to him. While he had no intention of going into business competition with Ewart Brindley, he knew that the time might come when a knowledge of mule packing could prove advantageous. So, leaving the organization of the escort to his subordinates, he was standing and watching the main preparations for the start of the return journey.

Taking everything into consideration, the Texian felt that he was entitled to grant himself a brief period of relaxation after the events of the past few days. Not only had he dealt with one positive and one potential threat to the consignment of caplocks, he had almost doubled the strength of its escort. Only time would tell whether the latter would be beneficial or not. He refused to worry about it at that moment.

Not one of the Red River Volunteer Dragoons had elected to follow Sergeant Benn, who had kept riding once he passed beyond the rim. Nor had a problem envisaged by Ole Devil arisen. Major Ludwig von Lowenbrau had waived the matter of his rank, stating that he placed himself and his men under the young captain's command until the delivery of the caplocks was completed. After which, the Prussian had gone on, he intended to offer to transfer himself and his company to the Texas Light Cavalry.

While von Lowenbrau had sounded sincere, Ole Devil had continued to be wary of him. However, there had been nothing about his behavior, or that of his men, to which exception could be taken. Not knowing how long they might have to wait for the mule train and wishing to keep the Dragoons out of mischief, Ole Devil had put them to work strengthening the defenses. While he was taking some well-earned and badly needed sleep, watched surreptitiously by Mannen Blaze, they had dug more rifle pits at the top of the hollow. The redhead had reported that, although there was some grumbling, they had carried out the duty in a satisfactory manner. By the middle of the afternoon, the chance of treachery had been greatly reduced.

Diamond-Hitch Brindley had wasted little time in utilizing the replacement bell-mare. Although her grandfather was being transported on a *travois** made by the Tejas packers, Joe Galton was sufficiently recovered to ride a horse. However, they had arrived at Santa Cristóbal Bay too late for there to be any point in loading the mules and moving out that day. So the girl and Ole Devil had agreed to bed down in the hollow for the night and set off early the following morning.

Looking around, Ole Devil could tell that what appeared to be a lot of confused activity taking place was all being carried out in a swift and purposeful manner which called for no action on his part. He was on the point of watching the

---

* *Travois: a primitive form of sledge, although not restricted to use on snow, constructed of two poles for shafts with a frame upon which the load is carried and drawn by a single animal.*

nearest mule packer, merely to find out how the work was performed, when something happened which prevented him from doing so.

"Riders coming, Cousin Devil!" Mannen Blaze called, speaking in what—for him—was considerable haste, having noticed the sentry on the rim giving one of the prearranged signals. Waving his hat from left to right in a series of double circular motions gave additional information. "Could be some of Tom Wolf's scouts headed in."

Partly to strengthen his force in case von Lowenbrau might still be contemplating treachery and knowing that the Tejas Indians would be even better at the duty than his own men, Ole Devil had sent Tom Wolf's scouts out to replace his pickets. As there was nobody else belonging to the party outside the hollow, in all probability the riders had been sent by Tom Wolf with urgent news. So the Texian wanted as little delay as possible in learning what it might be.

"I'll go up and meet them," Ole Devil decided, striding to where his linebacked dun gelding was standing saddled and ready for use. "Will you come with me, Major?"

"Thank you, Captain," von Lowenbrau answered, making just as quickly for his bay which was in an equal state of readiness.

Glancing around as he mounted, Ole Devil noticed that—like himself—all of the soldiers wore either cloak-coats or some other form of protective clothing. While fine, the weather was cold and damp. So he decided against telling them to remove the garments until he found out what the returning scouts had to say.

"Hey, Di!" the Texian called as he swung astride the dun's saddle, looking to where the girl was standing by her grandfather's *travois* and supervising the packers' work without needing to tell them anything. "Can you come with us, please?"

While the Tejas could speak a certain amount of English and some Spanish, only their leader was fluent in either and the Texian wanted a fuller report than he felt he could obtain by using those languages. Knowing that the girl was able to speak their tongue, in fact it could be termed her second language as she had been cared for by Wolf's squaw after the death of her parents, her presence would be of the greatest assistance.

"Be right with you," Di promised, knowing what Ole Devil had in mind. She directed a glare at her grandfather, who was trying to sit up, and went on, "Stay put, you're not going no place. Anyways, he wants somebody's can 'interpretate' Tejas for him properly. If you have to do anything, make sure the boys's *you* taught don't put the *aparejos** on upside down or backward."

Ignoring Brindley's spluttered response, the girl ran to her horse. Mounting, she set off after the two men. Catching up, she accompanied them toward the rim. On reaching it, they all gazed in the direction indicated by the sentry.

"Son-of-a-bitch!" Di yelled. "That's Tom Wolf. So whatever's fetched 'em must be real important."

"It would have to be for Tom to be doing it himself," Ole Devil admitted, taking note of the direction from which the two Indians were galloping. "Like the Comanches say, 'Bad news rides a fast horse.' And I'll take bets that I can guess what it is."

"Not with me!" Di stated emphatically.

"Or I," von Lowenbrau seconded, but was pleased by the thought that—although he had acted with efficiency up to that point—the Texian had omitted to take a basic military precaution before ascending to the rim.

"Damn it," the girl went on indignantly. "After us feeding

* *Aparejos: a type of pack saddle designed for heavy or awkwardly shaped loads.*

him and him putting the victuals down like they was going out of fashion, that son-of-a-bitching *mozo*'d lied to us."

"Or he was wrong about how far off they were," Ole Devil pointed out, thinking of the fear shown by Major Abrahan Phillipe Gonzales *de* Villena *y* Danvila's deserted servant—who was in the hollow and probably being better treated than in all his life—when first questioned. Stopping the dun, he dismounted and continued, "It doesn't matter which, but I go for my guess."

"You would," Di sniffed, joining the Texian on the ground. "Might just's well wait here 'n' find out just how bad it is."

"Let's hope it isn't as bad as you believe, Miss Brindley," von Lowenbrau suggested, also quitting his saddle.

"It'll likely be *worse*!" guessed the girl, knowing that they would have the answer within seconds.

"Them house-Indians* coming, *Diablo Viejo!*" announced Tom Wolf, translating Ole Devil's name into Spanish as he and the younger brave brought their mounts to rump-scraping halts before the trio. "Plenty of em. Maybe so twenty, thirty hands, with Mexican officers."

"How far off are they, Chief?" Di inquired, speaking Tejas.

"Except for their scouts, they're about two miles away," the Indian replied in the same language. "I collected Little Foot here on my way back and sent Son of the Wind to fetch in the rest of our men if there was time. I didn't figure *Diablo Viejo* would want them to know for sure I'd seen them and didn't wait to kill their scouts."

"Good thinking, Chief. That way there's just a chance they might go by without coming near enough to find us, although they're probably following my trail," Ole Devil remarked, when the girl had translated the report and, as Wolf started

* House-Indians: unlike the nomadic tribes, the Hopi, Zuni and kindred nations tended to make and live in permanent homes instead of transportable lodges or tipis.

speaking again, he could see the next information was displeasing her. "What is it, Di?"

"You don't need to count on 'em missing us, even if they wouldn't've seen the mule train's sign," the girl warned, anger flashing in her eyes. "That bitch de Moreau's with 'em, Tom recognized her from when they hit at Grandpappy Ewart 'n' Joe. She'll've been able to tell 'em just smack where we'll be."

"There's nothing more certain than *that*!" von Lowenbrau agreed, having heard of the abortive ambush and the escape of the woman in question. "It's a pity you didn't get her, Captain Hardin. She's probably the only one of them who would get a chance to tell the Mexicans what she knows."

"Blast it, Devil did all any man could and better'n many—!" Di protested.

"The major's right, though, they'd probably have shot any of the men they'd come across on sight," Ole Devil interrupted. "But, as she's sure to have told them, maybe we can turn it to our advantage. In fact, I think it already is!"

"How the hell do you make *that* out?" Di demanded and the Prussian showed just as great a lack of comprehension. "She'll bring 'em straight here, without them even having to do a mite of work cutting for sign."

"Yes," Ole Devil conceded. "But she doesn't know how many of us there are."

"She knows your whole company's here—" the girl began, then understanding came as it had with von Lowenbrau if the way he was nodding his head meant anything. "But she won't be taking your fellers into account, Major."

"Not unless they come across our tracks," the Prussian pointed out.

"That they not do, soldier-coat," Wolf put in, having been able to follow the conversation without difficulty and using it. He could speak good English if the need arose, but preferred to use his native tongue particularly when addressing white strangers.* "Coming way they are, they won't see 'em until they're out on this open ground here."

Listening to the Indian, Ole Devil had his own thoughts on the matter confirmed by an expert. While there were a fair amount of bushes, trees and other cover in the vicinity, through which even a large body of the enemy could pass undetected provided that they took precautions—which Wolf and his companion had not troubled to do—none of any consequence was available for a strip about two hundred yards wide extending from the cliffs and the rim of the bay. Having come in at a more acute angle than the Arizona Hopi *Activos* Regiment would be approaching, the tracks of the Red River Volunteer Dragoons were unlikely to be noticed until the more open terrain was entered. By then, if things could be arranged properly, it would be too late for the attackers to appreciate the danger.

"Whereabouts are their scouts, Tom?" Ole Devil asked.

"Maybe a mile back," Wolf replied, employing better English than when he had spoken to von Lowenbrau. "Not much more."

"Will they find your sign?" the Texian wanted to know.

"If they're any good, they will—and I think they are good," the Indian answered and, knowing that many settlers had small respect for his tribe's fighting qualities, went on, "We came back too fast to hide our tracks."

"I know," Ole Devil said, with a grin.

"I figured *you* did," Wolf stated, flickering a brief glance at

* Warrant and non-commissioned officers of the King's African Rifles also frequently had this trait. One with whom I worked for several months during the Mau Mau Uprising had been to England and taken the Drill Instructor's Course at the Brigade of Guards' Depot, Pirbright, Surrey, shortly after World War II. He could read and understand verbal instructions which were in English, but would only speak Swahili, the lingua franca of most race in Kenya, unless he knew the person he was addressing very well. J.T.E.

the Prussian although his words had been directed at the Texian.

"I hope they are good," Ole Devil declared, before the indignant von Lowenbrau could comment. "It'll be a help to us if they do cut your sign. They'll move even slower and give us more time to get ready. But we'd still better go down straightaway and get started at it, Major."

"Little Foot says do you want us to go and deal with their scouts?" Wolf translated after the younger brave had asked a question in tones of eager anticipation.

"Tell him I apologize for making him miss the chance to count coup, but they must be let come, see what we want them to see, then go to report," Ole Devil requested, mounting the dun. "But if they arrive before we're ready, they must be killed. Will you stay here, Chief, and attend to that for me, please?"

"You're leading this war party with Ewart and Joe shot," the Indian replied. "You tell us what you want doing and that is what we do."

"Gracias," Ole Devil answered, aware that he had been granted what amounted to an unqualified accolade, then he looked at the Prussian and, setting his horse moving, continued, "I hope your men see it the same way, Major."

Without elaborating upon his cryptic utterance, the Texian sent his dun loping down the slope. The girl and the Prussian followed him. Straightaway, von Lowenbrau discovered that he had not forgotten to take what would have been a necessary precaution when dealing with the Dragoons. Obviously he had known that he could count upon Mannen Blaze to assemble and form up the men ready to be put to whatever use the situation demanded. The two companies stood in separate groups and each man had a pair of the new caplocks to supplement their own arms.

"All right," Ole Devil said, leaping to the ground before

his mount had stopped and looking at the Dragoons. "I want all of you in the rifle pits you dug on top of the rim."

"Why *us*?" growled the man whom von Lowenbrau had promoted to replace Sergeant Benn, and there was a mumble of agreement from the other Dragoons.

"Because Captain Hardin has told you to do it!" the Prussian thundered, taking note of his men's reactions and seeing an opportunity to build up their resentment against the Texian.

"Yeah, but you're—" Sergeant Otis began, realizing that he and his companions would be in the forefront if—as seemed almost certain from what was happening—an enemy force was approaching.

"The protection of the arms is Captain Hardin's responsibility," von Lowenbrau interrupted, picking his words with care. "It is *he* who decides how it can best be carried out."

"Why that—!" Beauregard Rassendyll hissed and was on the point of going to support his friend.

"Stay put, Beau!" Mannen Blaze commanded, lounging in his usual fashion at the supercargo's side.

"Damn it, Mannen!" Rassendyll replied, glaring at the redhead. "Don't you see what he's trying to do?"

"I do," Mannen admitted languidly. "Only I reckon that Cousin Devil's eyesight's as good—and most likely better."

While the two young men had been speaking, another factor had entered the affair. Less perceptive than either with regard to the Prussian's motives, Di had listened to Otis's response to Ole Devil's orders. She found herself comparing their new helpers with Company "C" of the Texas Light Cavalry—and not to the former's advantage.

"There ain't no son-of-a-bitching time to stand arguing," the girl yelled angrily, glaring around the Dragoons. "But, happen you-all too scared to go up there, *I'll* come and hold your hands!"

"There'll be no need for that, Di," Ole Devil contradicted, although he was pleased by her spirited words. He could see that she had annoyed and, to a certain extent, shamed the Dragoons. "Mister Blaze, Tommy and I'll be with them."

"And I, Captain," von Lowenbrau stated, having no desire to lose the slight advantage he had gained from the sergeant's objections. "They're *my* company and as their commanding officer, it is my place to be with them."

"I'd agree, sir, but for one thing," Ole Devil countered politely. "You and your company aren't supposed to be here. Most of your men are wearing buckskin shirts like mine, so they'll pass as they won't be seen below the waist until it's too late. But having a strange officer could ruin everything."

"May I know what you have in mind, Captain?" the Prussian requested, neither making agreement nor refusal to the instructions.

"Certainly," Ole Devil replied. "Mister Blaze, Mister Rassendyll, Di, Joe, Sergeant Otis, Sergeant Dale, Corporal Smith, come and listen."

"By cracky, it could work!" Di enthused and could see that the men shared her sentiments, after the Texian had explained what he wanted to be done.

"You won't get no more arguments from me on that," Otis stated, although he was still aware that he and his men would be the first upon whom the attackers concentrated.

"I'll tell you something else there ain't going to be no son-of-a-bitching argument on either," Di declared, her expressive face set in lines of grim determination. "I'm going to be up there with you. De Moreau's with the greasers and, after all she's done to us, I figure me and her've got things to settle happen she comes close enough."

16

GIVE THEM THE CAPLOCKS

Colonel Otón Eugenio Alarcón *de* Reuda had one advantage over the officers under his command. While a wealthy *haciendero,* with a vast estate in Arizona, he had been a regular soldier for ten years in his youth. So he had felt that he was eminently qualified to make the most of the information which he had received from Madeline de Moreau.

Nor, on listening to the reports of his advance scouts, had the colonel been told anything to make him believe his summation of the situation was other than correct. Although he had had hardly any contact with the *gringo* rebels, few of whom had traveled so far west as his home, the stories he had heard of their traits and conduct had not left him with a high regard for their skill as fighting *soldiers.* Those who were guarding the consignment of arms might have taken a few precautions and they might know that the Arizona Hopi *Activos* Regiment were coming, but he still saw no cause for alarm.

Advancing with care and pondering upon how much better the terrain of East Texas was adapted to such tactics—although the cold and damp weather was less pleasant—than

most of the land in Arizona, Alarcón studied the state of the
enemies' defenses. They were obviously aware that his regiment was in the vicinity and were positioned to fight back.
However, he felt sure that he could exploit their weakness. It
stemmed from the climatic conditions' effect upon their
weapons. It was something which would not have such repercussions upon his men. Few, apart from the Mexican officers,
had firearms. Even the latter, appreciating the serious fault
which inflicted such weapons under the circumstances, would
be placing their reliance upon swords or sabers. Nor would
the lack of discipline which his military colleagues had declared was a characteristic of the *gringo* rebels make them as
effective as might otherwise have been the case.

Looking through his telescope at the figures assembled in
the rifle pits, the colonel made a rough estimate of their
numbers. Then he picked out their officers from the descrip-
tions he had been given by the woman who had been brought
to him by Major Abrahan Phillipe Gonzales *de* Villena *y*
Danvila. The tall, slim one with the face like *el Diablo* and
the burly redhead would be the primary targets for his men,
but he decided that the *gringo* in the well cut civilian clothing
and the small, yellow-skinned foreigner holding a bow and
arrows must also be regarded as of an equal priority. Possibly
the red-haired girl standing alongside the civilian could be
considered in a similar fashion, for Madeline de Moreau had
warned that she was as dangerous as any of her male companions. While the colonel was inclined to doubt the statement, he saw no reason to take chances. Nor did he want a
female prisoner, who might cause dissension among his
soldiers. Whether she was taken alive or not, the four men he
had selected must die as quickly as possible. Killing the leaders had always been sound strategy. With them gone, their
subordinates would have no guidance and be that much easier meat.

Satisfied with his examination, Alarcón closed the telescope and glanced at the Hopi Indian who had brought him to the point of observation. They withdrew with a care equal to that displayed as they moved in and he was confident that they had come and gone without the Texians being aware of their visit. Collecting their horses, they rode back to where the rest of the regiment was waiting. He was confident of success and pleased with the thought of the acclaim which would be forthcoming in its wake.

Not that the colonel underestimated the fighting qualities of individual *gringos,* having heard of what had happened in San Antonio de Bexar the previous year.* Of course, the Texians who were involved then had been more numerous and commanded by older, more experienced leaders. However, the rebels had also appeared to have scored a number of minor victories in skirmishes during the early days of the rebellion. What was more, although they were withdrawing from the west, he could understand and even approve of Major General Samuel Houston's reluctance to meet a larger army in an open confrontation unless on favorable terms.

For all that, unlike their fellow rebels in the earlier victories—who were fighting hit-and-run on the offensive—the men he had been studying were outnumbered and acting in a defensive capacity. Alarcón felt sure that the rank and file of the company would appreciate that their inexperienced commanding officer had not even left them with the means for rapid flight if their position should prove untenable. There had been no sign of their horses, which therefore could not be closer than fifty yards away and below the rim overlooking Santa Cristóbal Bay. The officer might even have arranged it that way, as the colonel knew he personally would in similar

* *This is the incident referred to in the footnote on page 38.*

circumstances, to ensure that the men stood their ground to the bitter end.

"Very well, gentlemen—and you, *Señora* de Moreau," Alarcón announced, looking at the three majors and nine lieutenants who were gathered about the woman. His gaze went next to the leaders of the Hopi Indians who were serving as non-commissioned officers over the rest of the braves. "All is as Chief Jesus† told us. We can follow the kind of action which I outlined when I heard our first scouts' reports."

There was a brief rumble of interest and delight at the colonel's news. The commanding officers of the three companies who were present had approved of the tentative plan which he had made, provided that it should be workable. Nor could the Hopi war leaders, who were practical and experienced tacticians, find fault with the reasoning behind it. However, none of the lieutenants gave the tactics a great deal of thought. Each was more interested in the prospect of going into action, with the attendant possibility of outdoing the others and winning Madeline de Moreau's approbation.

The one person who might have shown the main flaws in the scheme failed to do so.

Having been admitted into the councils of war which were caused by her arrival and news, although noticing that she had been kept under observation at all times, the woman had approved of all she had heard. She had warned that the Mexicans should not take the Texians' leader too lightly, without being too determined in stressing just how competent he had proved to be. While the regiment consisted of ten fifty-strong companies, a useful system in that it allowed a greater number of promotions, seven had been left three days' ride to the south. So she had not wished to have her revenge delayed

† *Pronounced "Hey-Soos."*

while reinforcements could be summoned because Alarcón decided the enemy was too dangerous for his force to handle.

"You were correct about the mule train having been brought here, *señora,*" the colonel went on, causing the junior officers to scatter like flies frightened from a pool of honey. "Or at least, the number of men in the rifle pits indicates that it is."

On telling how her ambush had failed, laying all the blame on her now scattered or dead associates, Madeline had warned that there was a possibility that the two sections of the enemies' party were reunited. Although she had not lingered in the vicinity of San Phillipe, she had felt sure that the bell-mare had been replaced. In which case, she could count upon Ole Devil Hardin and Diamond-Hitch Brindley to waste no time in putting the new animal to use. For all that, it rankled to learn that the young couple had once again proved to be so capable and efficient. However, the woman found some consolation in considering that both of them would be at Santa Cristóbal Bay, and the full strength of Company "C" of the Texas Light Cavalry and the Brindleys' Tejas mule packers were less than half the number of the Arizona Hopi *Activos* Regiment.

"That will save us going looking for them," Villena called out and the other officers mumbled their agreement.

"The time has come for us to ride, gentlemen," Alarcón stated. "But I don't need to warn any of you to use cold steel and not to fall into *their* error."

"May I accompany you, Colonel?" Madeline inquired.

"It won't be any place for a lady, *señora,*" Alarcón pointed out.

"Nor do I expect it to be," the woman declared and her emotions turned her face ugly. "But they murdered my husband and I have a score to settle with them."

For a few seconds, Alarcón did not offer to reply. While he

had read the woman's identification pass, he was not familiar with *Presidente* Antonio Lopez de Santa Anna's signature. So he could not tell whether the document was genuine or not. However, he was aware of what his fate would be if it should be authentic and he had not honored it. Nor would his future career be improved if he allowed a friend of el *Presidente* to be harmed.

"Very well, *señora*," the colonel finally said. "You may come. But it must be on the understanding that you do so at your own risk and knowing there will be a very great element of danger."

"That is fully understood and accepted, Colonel," Madeline replied, her hatred for the girl and the Texian driving out any thought of the perils she would be facing. She nodded to the listening officers, going on, "These gentlemen are witnesses that I insisted upon going and that no blame shall attach itself to *you* in the event of my being killed or injured."

"My thanks, *señora,* and well said," Alarcón answered, but decided that precautions might still be in order. "I must only ask that you stay close to me—"

"Perhaps you'd be good enough to put me under Major Villena *y* Danvila's care, *señor,*" the woman suggested, guessing that—having captured the leader of the Texians and allowing him to escape—the officer in question would be the best choice for her purpose. He would want to remove the stain on his reputation by killing Ole Devil Hardin and would put her in the best position to achieve the same end. "If he doesn't object, that is."

"It will be my privilege, *señora,*" Villena stated.

"Very well," the colonel authorized, realizing that the major could be made to bear the brunt of the recriminations if anything should befall the female renegade. "I trust you will take no unnecessary chances, *señora*?"

"I've no wish to be killed, Colonel," Madeline replied.

On rejoining their men, the officers removed the outer clothing which they had donned to combat the inclement weather. Although travel-stained, their uniforms looked martial and impressive; particularly when compared with the way the men under their command were dressed.

Wanting a greater freedom of movement, Madeline peeled off her cloak-coat. Taking the "Pepperbox" from the pocket, she tucked its barrel into her waistband. Then she handed the heavy outer garment to one of the small party of *mozos* who were waiting to take care of the officers' property. Having done so, she joined Villena and his lieutenants.

With his force mounted, Alarcón gave the order to advance. Following his plan, each company formed into three ranks. The youngest braves and the lieutenants were in front, with the older warriors and senior officers bringing up the rear. Nor had either the junior officers nor the Hopis seen anything unusual in the formation. To the Indians' way of thinking, such an arrangement was not only logical but honorable* and such of the lieutenants as bothered to give it any consideration accepted that it was being done to satisfy the preferences of the men under their command.

Madeline de Moreau was not alone in feeling that such an arrangement had merit. Seeing the advantages, the colonel and the three majors had been only too happy to go along with the Hopis' tradition. It gave them a greater chance of survival and the woman saw it in the same light.

Although the colonel and Chief Jesus had contrived to reach a point of vantage from which they could study the enemy without being detected, they had realized that there

---

* As with the majority of Indian tribes, the Hopis considered that the older and more experienced warriors had already had many opportunities to earn acclaim and loot. So they could allow those who were less fortunate to have the first opportunities by leading the attack.

was no chance of such a large body of men meeting with
equal success. Nor did he mean for them to waste time trying. Instead, they were heading straight for their objective.
Once the Texians saw them coming, he would be able to find
out if a very important aspect of his strategy was correct. He
hoped that it would be, for he had used it as a major argument when the dangers of a frontal attack upon what would
probably be prepared positions had been raised.

Before the Hopis were within a hundred yards of the strip
of almost open land, the defenders had seen them. Finding
themselves located, the front rank let out whoops and urged
their horses forward at an increased pace.

Looking between the men ahead of him, Alarcón gave a
sigh of relief. Just as he had anticipated, instead of waiting to
deliver volley firing when the Indians reached the fringe of
the sheltered terrain—which would have proved advantageous to him, provided the other factor happened—first one
and then many of the other men in the pits began to open
fire.

Or tried to!

Only a few of the rifles spoke!

The remainder proved to be suffering from a terribly dangerous fault of the flintlock mechanism under such climatic
conditions.† Having been affected by the damp air, the powder in the priming pans was failing to ignite and set off the
main charges in the barrels.

Seeing that their colonel's prediction was justified even the
more cautious of the older braves cast aside their doubts.
When rifle after rifle misfired, they added their war whoops
to those of the leading ranks and signaled for their mounts to
go faster.

Dashing through the bushes and other cover, the three

† *Another example of just how serious the flintlocks' fault could be is given
in* OLE DEVIL AT SAN JACINTO.

companies were prepared to launch a determined and, what they felt sure would be, an unstoppable charge. With the way the Texians' weapons were failing to function, they could have done little to save themselves even if they had been sufficiently well disciplined to wait and deliver a volley.

Or so thought the attacking force.

Although the attackers did not realize it, they were being lured into a trap!

Ole Devil Hardin had been counting upon the Red River Volunteer Dragoons contingent's lack of discipline to help him spring it. That was why he had selected them to occupy the rifle pits. For the success of his scheme, he needed men upon whom he could rely implicitly below the rim and concealed from the enemies' view.

However, while guessing that any attempt at volley firing would be doomed to failure where the Dragoons were concerned, Ole Devil had given one command to them. Only a few owned percussion-fired weapons and he had insisted that they employed their personal arms before bringing the caplocks he had lent to them into action. He had also threatened to shoot any man who attempted to touch the new rifles before he gave permission. It said much for the respect, or fear, which he inspired among them that not one had offered to go against his orders even after their pieces failed to function.

Knowing what was at stake, Di, Mannen, Tommy Okasi, Rassendyll and Joe Galton had not fired so much as a shot between them. While the discovery of a rifle which could keep on pumping out lead without apparently needing to be reloaded might have had a salutary effect upon the Indians,* from the defenders' point of view, Mannen doubted whether any of them would notice it in the excitement and confusion

*Just how great an effect the firepower of the Browning Slide Repeating Rifles had under suitable conditions is told in GET URREA.

of the mass charge. So he was saving the five bullets until they could be put to a more useful purpose. Nor was the little Oriental using his bow, preferring to economize where the arrows were concerned.

Reaching the open ground, the Hopis and their Mexican officers made an awesome sight. Brandishing lances, throwing sticks, bows and arrows, or in the lieutenants' cases, some kind of a sword, they swept onward.

"Now!" Ole Devil roared, swinging the butt of his Browning Slide Repeating rifle to his shoulder. "Give them the caplocks, Dragoons!"

Eagerly and with great relief, the enlisted men in the pits discarded their own arms to snatch up the first of their reserve rifles. Every one of them hoped that the caplocks would prove more effective than the weapons which had failed to function.

However, the sight of the Dragoons changing rifles was not the attackers' main source of consternation. To their amazement, many more *gringos* began to appear over what the majority of the Mexicans and Indians had assumed to be the edge of the cliff. Each of the newcomers was holding a rifle ready for use and had a second, with a bayonet attached, suspended by an improvised sling across his back.

Shock and alarm burst through Alarcón as he realized that he had been tricked into greatly underestimating the number of the enemy. There was, however, no time for him to wonder if his informant had been a party to the deception.* Other matters of more immediate importance were demanding his undivided attention, particularly the way in which the newcomers were behaving. From all appearances, they were

---

* *Madeline de Moreau had not deliberately misled Colonel Alarcón about the Texians' armament. The information which she and her husband had received was merely that a shipment of new rifles was to arrive and the nature of their mechanisms had not been mentioned.*

far better disciplined than the occupants of the pits. Although they might not be acting with the puppetlike precision of some of the crack European regiments he had heard and read about, they advanced from the rim and, halting in a fairly straight line, lifted their rifles to the aiming position so nearly simultaneously as to be impressive—

And, but for the lethal fault of the flintlock mechanism, frightening.

Alarcón and his men doubted whether more than a fraction of the weapons being pointed at them would perform in a more satisfactory manner than those of their previous assailants.

"Fire!" bellowed Major Ludwig von Lowenbrau, having been assigned to perform the duty as he could see when the men from below the rim were ready whereas Ole Devil could not without looking away from the enemy.

Over sixty rifles roared and Tommy Okasi's long bow twanged in a ragged, but adequately concentrated volley. It was followed by the shots from those of the Dragoons who had been less speedy in exchanging weapons.

Already halfway across the open strip, the tightly packed ranks of the Arizona Hopi *Activos* Regiment's three companies were ideally positioned to be caught by the holocaust, and they suffered grievously. Horses and men went down like wheat before a mower's scythe.

Being in the forefront of the attackers, not one of the Mexican lieutenants survived the onslaught. Their colonel had not been alone in appreciating the tactical and moral value of removing officers and the Texians had acted accordingly. What was more, practically every member of the front rank felt the effects of the volley. Although they bore the brunt of the casualties, some of the bullets found billets in the men who were following them after having passed between—or through—their bodies. In fact, those who were behind horses which were struck down might have counted themselves fortunate. At something around a hundred yards, the lead could not pass through the length of the animal's body and emerge to fly on with sufficient velocity to claim a second victim.

Just how well Ole Devil had laid his plans was shown by the success which his party had attained. With the single, well-delivered volley, the assault by the much larger force had been disrupted and brought to a halt. What was more, the effect went even further than he had anticipated. He had not suspected that the Mexican colonel would have counted upon his men being armed with flintlocks and that these would misfire in the damp air.

Nor were the Texians finished!

Without waiting for or needing orders, the members of Company "C" dropped the empty rifles and began to liberate the second weapons from across their backs. The Dragoons were also making the necessary adjustments to allow them to continue the bombardment. While they were doing so, Ole Devil, Mannen and Tommy made use of the Brownings' and the bow's capabilities for rapid reloading and sought to select the best targets among the mill of rearing, swerving, hopelessly entangled and confused riders.

Ole Devil toppled one of the majors. A brave passing between them saved Alarcón's life by intercepting the bullet which Mannen had thrown at him. However, Chief Jesus was less fortunate. Having contrived to keep some kind of control over his war pony, he emerged through the scattered dead or wounded animals and men to try and rally the rest. Before he could do so, he was transfixed by the little Oriental's arrow and joined many of his braves on the ground.

To give the Hopis their due, while realizing that their war medicine—the belief in which no amount of Christian mission indoctrination succeeded in wiping out—had failed, some of them tried to fight back.

Before the Texians could fire a second time, a throwing stick* spun through the air and struck von Lowenbrau's head and he went down.

Holding her second rifle cocked and ready, Di was scanning the confused mass before her in the hope of locating Madeline de Moreau when she heard a cry of pain from alongside her.

Having emptied both his rifles, Rassendyll had set down the second where it would be readily available if he required the bayonet that was attached to it and was reaching for the Croodlom & Co. "Duck Foot" Mob Pistol which was laying close by. Before his fingers could grasp the butt, an arrow struck him in the shoulder. He could not restrain his agonized exclamation. Grabbing ineffectually at the shaft which was protruding from his flesh, he spun around to stumble against the rear of the pit.

Two of the Dragoons and four members of Company "C" were also struck by the Hopis' missiles, while others had narrow escapes as arrows or throwing sticks whizzed by them. However, such reprisals—only one member of each party received a fatal injury—were nothing compared to the slaughter which had been dealt out already—

And that which was about to be inflicted!

Less than twenty seconds after the supercargo had been

* The throwing stick of the Hopi and related tribes of North American Indians is a similar device to the war and hunting boomerang of the Australian aborigines, but is neither designed nor expected to return to the thrower if it misses its target. This does not make it any less effective as a weapon. American author, Daniel Mannix—who, in Chapter 7, "The Boomerang— The Stick That Kills" of his book A SPORTING CHANCE covers the subject thoroughly—has thrown one a distance of five hundred and forty feet and it still retained sufficient force at the end to crack an inch-thick limb of a tree.

wounded, although too late to prevent it from happening, Sergeant Dale gave the order and Company "C" turned loose their second fusilade. Nor had the slight delay while the non-com had waited—being unaware that von Lowenbrau was indisposed—reduced its effectiveness. In fact, it proved to be just as devastating and even more potent than its predecessor.

Once again, the deadly tempest of lead assailed the Hopis. Any who had managed to evade the confusion and were trying to continue the attack were selected as targets. The others were hit, or missed, by random shooting as the fates directed. Many fell, including the second major who had come to the fore and was heading toward the rifle pits.

However, Madeline and Villena survived both of the vollies. Being cautious and knowing that his uniform made him an easily distinguishable target, the major had contrived to keep as many bodies as possible between himself and the enemy. He did not wish to let his former captive or the strange little foreigner pick him out for revenge. On her part, the woman was aware that Di Brindley would not hesitate to kill her. So she had allowed the men to draw ahead and had followed ready to grab any opportunity which was presented, or let them take care of the objects of her hatred.

While the Hopis were far from being cowards, there was a limit to how much punishment they were willing to take when there seemed little hope of returning it. What was more, a number of the leaders had fallen and the rest saw no reason to throw their lives away. So they turned and fled, scattering in every direction save toward their assailants.

Seeing what was happening, the woman and Villena followed the Hopis' example. They went independently, neither giving even a thought to the other or to the men whom each had helped send to their deaths.

At the sight of Madeline dashing away, Di threw a shot

after her and missed. Growling a curse, the girl dropped her empty weapon and looked at Rassendyll. Experienced in such matters, she knew that the wound was not desperately dangerous.

"I'll send the doc to you, Beau!" Di promised, grabbing up the mob pistol. "And I'll borrow this seeing's you'll not be needing it."

With that, the girl bounded up the rear slope of the pit, which had been dug at such an angle as to facilitate a rapid departure. Already the men of Company "C" were charging forward to use their bayonets and deal with the unhorsed, but uninjured Hopis. So she knew that she was not leaving the supercargo defenseless while she pursued the urgent matter demanding her attention.

The Tejas left to look after the mules and, if need be, to destroy the consignment by blowing it up. However, half a dozen of them stood just below the rim holding several saddled horses. One was Ewart Brindley's big *grulla** gelding, selected by the girl as her own mount was tired from the strenuous activity of the previous few days. Running to it, she used her empty hand to grab the reins from the young brave. Swinging astride the saddle, she set the spirited animal into motion and went like a bat out of hell in the direction from which she had come.

* *Grulla: a bluish-gray horse much the same color as a sandhill crane.*

17
THAT'S ANOTHER I OWE YOU, DE MOREAU

Madeline de Moreau was traveling at a good rate, but she was not afraid of being followed by the Texians after her original near panic had subsided. From various noises which had reached her ears, she had concluded that close-quarters fighting was taking place. So her enemies would be too occupied in dealing with the surviving Hopis to pursue her. Having made her deduction, she saw no reason to keep on pushing her horse at such a speed. It had seen much use recently and she wished to conserve its energy in case of emergency. What was more, she needed it to carry her to safety.

After what had happened on the cliffs above Santa Cristóbal Bay, the woman felt it would be advisable to avoid further contact with the Arizona Hopi *Activos* Regiment. Once the remaining companies heard of their companions' fate, they might believe she had brought it about deliberately. Nor would any of the survivors who had fled be more inclined to regard her favorably. So she must seek out some other Mexican force and try to persuade its officers to offer her protection from the Indians in addition to striking at the consignment of caplocks.

Bitter rage surged through the woman as she realized that the objects of her hatred had not only survived her wrath, but had once again got the better of her. The emotion was so intense that, at first, she took no notice of the sound of a horse approaching rapidly from her rear. Becoming aware of it, she looked back expecting to find one of the Hopis was following. Dangerous as that might have been under the circumstances, she learned she was wrong in her assumption; but the pursuer posed an even greater threat.

Perhaps an Indian would have been more interested in escaping than repaying her for what she had helped to bring about, but that did not apply to Diamond-Hitch Brindley.

The pistol in the girl's right hand was grim evidence of her intentions!

Letting out a shriek of combined fury and fright, the woman turned her gaze to the front and slammed her heels savagely against the flanks of her mount. Jabbed by her spurs' sharp rowels, it bounded forward with a force which almost caused her to drop the single-barreled pistol she had drawn at the start of the charge and had not yet replaced in its saddle holster. However, she contrived to retain her grip on the butt and started to urge her horse to go even faster.

Having set off in the general direction taken by Madeline, ignoring the hand-to-hand fighting by the men, Di had soon caught sight of her. Excellently mounted on a horse which was comparatively fresh, the girl had not doubted that she could overtake the woman. However, in case there might be shooting at other than close quarters, she had decided against depending upon the weapon she had borrowed from Beauregard Rassendyll. Taking advantage of a refinement he had had applied, she hung it on her saddle horn by the rawhide loop which was threaded through a ring on the butt. Then she had drawn a pistol from the brace which were holstered on her rig. With the heavy caliber flintlock in her hand, she felt that she could deal with any situation that might arise.

Oblivious of everything except one another, guiding their mounts almost instinctively through fairly open bush speckled country, the girl and the woman galloped in a southwesterly direction. The latter was fleeing with the fear of death as her goad and the former rode just as recklessly, spurred on by a desire to kill.

Almost a mile fell behind the pursued and the pursuer!

Slowly, but inexorably, Di's big *grulla* was closing the gap between them!

Having noticed this, in rapid glances taken to her rear whenever the opportunity had arisen, Madeline tried desperately to improve the situation. Gallantly as her flagging and lathered mount responded to the punishment she was inflicting with her spurs, it failed to draw away.

Driving the horse up a gentle slope, with slightly less than a hundred yards separating it and the *grulla,* the woman felt it reeling. Just as it reached the top, it stumbled and almost threw her. This time, she lost her hold on the pistol and, as it flew from her fingers, the exhausted animal started to collapse. Sobbing in alarm, she flung herself from the saddle. Not until her momentum had carried her several steps forward did she realize that she had left the weapon's mate in its holster on her saddle. Nor did she feel that the "Pepperbox" would serve her needs under the circumstances.

Turning around, Madeline almost hurled herself toward the stricken animal. She could see Di charging through the bushes and the sight gave her an inducement for extra speed. Snatching out the pistol, she prepared to fight for her life. Cocking and sighting it, she squeezed the trigger. With a crack, it vomited out its load. Although the bullet failed to contact the girl, it drove into the *grulla*'s chest.

A superb rider, Di felt the lead's impact and her mount

going down. She knew what she must do. Liberating her feet from the stirrup irons, she kicked her right leg forward and over the *grulla*'s head. Jumping clear, she alighted without being trapped by the falling animal. Unfortunately, she landed upon a piece of uneven ground. While it threw her off balance, she neither fell nor lost her pistol. However, before she had recovered her equilibrium, she saw that her troubles were far from over.

Hurling the empty pistol aside, the woman looked for its mate. She discovered that it had buried the tip of its barrel into the ground. So there was a chance that the muzzle was plugged and it would not be usable. Instead of wasting time in checking, she snatched the "Pepperbox" from her waistband. It was one of the best models available, percussion fired and double action in operation. While its mechanism did not allow for such rapid shooting as would later and better designed revolvers,* it still permitted a rate of fire far in excess of any contemporary handgun.

"That's another I owe you, de Moreau!" Di shrieked, glancing at the dying *grulla*.

Spitting out obscenities in French and English, Madeline brought up the "Pepperbox" with both hands. However, she knew its limitations and started to move closer. For all her knowledge, she could not refrain from chancing a shot when she saw the girl was drawing a bead on her. Not surprisingly, considering her weapon's rudimentary sights, she missed. At first, rage caused her to overlook her peril. Even as the realization struck her, she could tell—although they were still

---

* *The fastest recorded rate of fire for a manually operated double action mechanism occurred on January 23, 1834, at the Company "K," 163rd Infantry's Armory, Lewiston, Montana. Using a .38 caliber Smith & Wesson Model 1899 revolver, No. 640792, Ed. McGivern fired five shots into a playing card at eighteen feet in two-fifths of a second; not, of course, starting with it holstered.*

too far apart to make out the actual movements—that Di was squeezing the pistol's trigger.

Confident that she was holding true on the center of the woman's breast, the girl sensed rather than noticed that the flintlock's hammer was pivoting toward the frizzen plate. It struck, striking sparks that fell into the pan as the plate hinged back under the impact.

There was no other result!

In her eagerness to settle accounts with Madeline, Di had fallen into the error which Colonel Alarcón had hoped would afflict her companions. Either that, or the roughness of her landing when quitting the falling horse had jolted the priming powder from the pan. Whichever it might be, she was in dire and deadly peril.

Again the woman's weapon cracked, its comparatively light powder charge ejecting a .34 caliber ball which stirred the girl's red locks in passing. Continuing her advance, Madeline drew back the trigger, which turned the next barrel into the battery and cocked the hammer. Despite being taken on the move, the third shot came even closer to achieving her purpose.

Di saw the puff of white smoke well from the uppermost muzzle of her assailant's weapon, then felt as if a red-hot iron had been pressed lightly against her left shoulder. Pain slammed her into a fuller awareness of her predicament. She had heard of "Pepperboxes" and guessed that the woman must be using something of the kind.

What was more, de Moreau did not intend to miss, or merely score a flesh wound, next time!

Coming to a halt, the woman took a more careful aim than would be possible—even employing both hands—while on the move. After the first three attempts, Di had developed a *very* healthy respect for her marksmanship.

Accepting that there was only one hope for her, the girl

spun around and ran toward her horse. With each step, she expected to feel lead driving into or flying past her.

Sighting at the middle of the girl's back, Madeline was confident that she could send the bullet into it. Set free by the rearward movement of the sear, the hammer descended—

And produced no better result than Di had achieved with the flintlock!

But for a different reason!

Madeline had fallen foul of the deadly flaw to which Ole Devil Hardin had known percussion-fired "Pepperboxes" were prone. Unlike the revolvers that would soon succeed and eventually replace them, which had the caps situated horizontally at the rear of the cylinder, the formation of the barrels caused the cap-nipples to be placed on top and vertically. So, unless seated very firmly, when a barrel was at the lowest point of the axis around which it revolved the cap frequently fell off.

To give the woman credit, she realized what had caused the misfire and understood how to correct it. Unfortunately, neither realization nor understanding came quite quickly enough. Even as she started to press at the trigger, she saw the girl diving over the horse.

Although Di was wondering what had prevented Madeline from shooting, she made no attempt to find out before she had rearmed herself. Remembering what had happened with its mate, she ignored her second pistol. Instead, she jerked free Rassendyll's weapon. The Mob Pistol had started its life as a flintlock, but he had had it altered to handle percussion caps by a master gunsmith in Louisiana.

Praying that the artisan had carried out the modification satisfactorily, although she did not put it into those exact words, the girl drew back the single hammer which served the quadruple barrels. Even as she noticed the brass cap sitting so comfortingly on its nipple, she heard footsteps drawing rapidly closer to the horse behind which she was crouching. Obviously the woman was gambling upon her second pistol producing no better result than its mate and was approaching for the kill.

"Have you got a surprise—" Di began, but the thought was cut off when she came very near to death.

Once again, Madeline was firing on the move. However, her bullet did no more than nick the lobe of the girl's ear; which was only a matter of pure chance. She had aimed with all possible care, but her heavy breathing had spoiled what should have been a fatal shot.

Thrusting herself into a kneeling posture, Di swung around the Mob Pistol in both her hands. Even so, Madeline was already squeezing at the "Pepperbox's" trigger and looming at such a proximity that she would not be likely to miss again.

There was no time for the girl to take a careful aim, but the weapon she held had been designed to remove the need for that. Slanting it in the woman's general direction, she cut loose.

Touched off by the impact of the hammer, the percussion cap ignited the priming charge in the chamber which was connected to all four barrels. There was a sullen roar louder than any other pistol or rifle could produce and a quartet of .45 caliber balls spread fanlike through the air from their respective muzzles. Madeline was so close that she took three of them in a line across her bosom. Shock and agony slammed her backward, with the "Pepperbox" flying from her grasp as she went down.

Hooves thundered from behind the girl. With a cold sensation of apprehension, she realized that she did not have a firearm with which to defend herself if the riders—she knew that there must be at least two—were enemies. Swinging around and driving herself erect, she dropped the Mob Pistol which had saved her life and sent her right hand flying to the knife sheathed upon her belt. The gesture proved to be unnecessary. A sigh of relief broke from her as she recognized the three men who were bearing down so rapidly upon her.

"See you got her, Di," Mannen Blaze remarked, in his invariable languid manner.

"That's what I come out here for," the girl answered, throwing a glance at the lifeless body of the woman who had caused them so much trouble and danger. Then she turned her gaze to Ole Devil and Tommy Okasi, both of whom were displaying—if only a good friend could have seen it—satisfaction and pleasure at finding her alive. "I'd say you boys've handed them Hopis their needings."

"We have," Ole Devil Hardin confirmed. "So now perhaps we can get the caplocks on their way to General Houston."*

* How the caplocks were delivered and the use to which they were put is told in OLE DEVIL AT SAN JACINTO.

J.T. EDSON

Brings to Life the Fierce and Often Bloody Struggles of the Untamed West

__THE BAD BUNCH	20764-9	$3.50
__THE FASTEST GUN IN TEXAS	20818-1	$3.50
__NO FINGER ON THE TRIGGER	20749-5	$3.50
__SLIP GUN	20772-X	$3.50
__TROUBLED RANGE	20773-8	$3.50
__JUSTICE OF COMPANY Z	20858-0	$3.50
__COMANCHE	20930-7	$3.50
__A MATTER OF HONOR	20936-6	$3.50
__WACO RIDES IN	21019-4	$3.50
__BLOODY BORDER	21031-3	$3.50
__ALVIN FOG, TEXAS RANGER	21034-8	$3.50
__OLE DEVIL AT SAN JACINTO	21040-2	$3.50
__HELL IN PALO DURO	21037-2	$3.50
__OLE DEVIL AND THE MULE TRAIN	21036-4	$3.50
__VIRIDIAN'S TRAIL	21039-9	$3.99

FLOATING OUTFIT SERIES

__THE HIDE AND TALLOW MEN	20862-9	$3.50
__THE NIGHTHAWK	20726-6	$3.50
__RENEGADE	20964-1	$3.50
__GO BACK TO HELL	21033-X	$3.50